Easter, 1987.

Sweet Dreams
The Bedtime Story Book

Dear Christopher,

May you always enjoy your stories in the wonderful world of make-believe.

Grandpa was with me when we selected this book for you.

Love, Grandma June

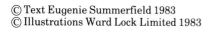

First published in Great Britain in 1983
by Ward Lock Limited, London,
a Pentos Company.
This edition published by Gallery Books,
an imprint of W.H. Smith Publishers Inc.,
112 Madison Avenue, New York, New York 10016.

Printed and bound in Italy by Sagdos SpA

ISBN 0-8317-8578-0

Sweet Dreams

The Bedtime Story Book

Stories by Eugenie Summerfield

Illustrated by Robin Lawrie

GALLERY BOOKS

An Imprint of W. H. Smith Publishers Inc.

112 Madison Avenue

New York City 10016

Contents

Mr Wonderful's Grey Cloud

'Not a cloud in sight! This really won't do,' said the Queen impatiently, looking up at the clear blue sky. She frowned, as she looked from her window over the smooth lawns and magnificent gardens towards the new lily-pond. There was no water in the pond because the Queen had given orders that it should only be filled with the purest rain-water. But, for several days now, not a drop of rain had fallen.

'I *must* have rain-water in my lily-pond,' declared the Queen. 'No other kind of water will do.'

She closed the window with a slam.

'We must have some rain,' said the Queen.

Mr Wonderful's bushy white eyebrows shot up in surprise.

'Rain, Your Majesty? But we had some rain only the other week and the farmers aren't complaining.'

'That was *before* my lily-pond was finished. Now it is ready and must be filled with crystal clear rain-water. So you are going to make a rain cloud for me!'

'Me, Your Majesty?'

'Yes, you!' she snapped.

Mr Wonderful hurried off to the Library, as fast as his old legs would carry him, and got down all the books he could find about rain-making machines. The whole morning he was hard at work, drawing lots of diagrams on the backs of old envelopes and spilling cups of tea all over them; hammering and sawing bits and pieces, then dropping the hammer on his toe, once or twice. But, early in the afternoon, back he went to the Queen, triumphantly pushing before him a strange-looking contraption on wheels.

'My rain-making machine, Your Majesty!' he announced proudly.

'Humph, let's hope it works,' replied the Queen doubtfully.

Mr Wonderful didn't seem too sure either.

'I'm almost sure it will,' he said cautiously, 'but it may make rather a lot of smoke just at first, when it's switched on.'

The strange contraption was taken across to the far side of the Palace lawns and a crowd of people gathered round – at a safe distance of course – to see what would happen.

Mr Wonderful pushed a knob here, turned a handle there and with a 'BANG' and a 'WHIRR-URR', smoke started to stream from the machine and spread across the lawns like a dense fog. When at last the smoke drifted away and everyone had stopped coughing, there up in the bright sky was a small, rather raggedy, grey cloud.

Now Mr Wonderful was not at all certain if his machine had made it or not; anyway, he felt sure the Queen would be pleased about it. But with a gasp of horror, the Queen suddenly exclaimed,

'The Royal Soccer Game! Why didn't someone remind me? We can't have this afternoon's game ruined by rain! Mr Wonderful – get rid of that nasty rain cloud at once.'

'B-b-but, Your Majesty . . .' spluttered Mr Wonderful.

'There are no "buts" about it! Hurry!' she commanded.

So, with a sad sigh, off went Mr Wonderful to find a rain-removing spell.

Meanwhile high above, the grey cloud uncurled itself, stretched, and began to spread itself over the clear sky.

'Oh . . . oh!' groaned the spectators, as they looked up at the cloud in dismay. 'Just look at that grey cloud. It'll ruin our soccer game.'

The grey cloud moved further over the sky.

'I don't like the look of that cloud,' said one white-clad player to another, as the teams walked on to the field to start their game.

The cloud was close to the sun now and, for one brief moment, was transformed from an ugly grey to a glowing gold.

'Go away! You're not wanted here,' said the sun.

From the cloud a tear-drop fell.

'A drop of rain,' complained a fat lady wearing a flowered hat. 'Oh, what a nuisance my hat will be ruined.'

A gentle breeze began to stir.

'Perhaps this wind will blow the cloud away,' someone suggested.

Another tear-drop fell. Then,

'Come, climb on my back,' whispered the wind to the cloud, 'and I'll take you far, far away.'

SWI-SH-SH went the wind and away sailed the cloud, over fields all green and golden, over dark-green forests and deep, blue seas.

'P-OU-FF. You've grown so big and heavy now, that I can't carry you much further,' breathed the wind. 'There's land ahead and I'll take you as far as those mountains.'

Beyond the mountains, in fields which were parched and bare, there worked an old woman. She was poor and very tired, for she had been working since early morning.

She sighed and stopped to rest awhile.

'Unless there is rain soon, the crops won't grow and my children will go hungry.' And she began to cry.

But just at that moment, the wind flung the cloud against the mountains and a most wonderful change took place.

From the cloud
began to fall
thousands of
shimmering
glimmering
raindrops.

The parched earth greedily drank in the precious rain. The old woman laughed with joy. Children came running out, shouting and singing, as they tried to catch the falling raindrops. No one noticed the grey cloud, which danced off and disappeared into the sky again.

Four and Twenty Blackbirds

All around the Palace, the birds were singing, singing with all their might.

'Just like a beautiful lullaby!' sighed the King. He pulled the bedclothes more tightly round him, closed his eyes and fell asleep. It was five o'clock in the morning, but the King didn't sleep much in the night, so he loved the early morning music of the birds to lull him to sleep until breakfast-time.

Now there was someone who did *not* like to hear the birds singing. This was Mr McFie, the King's Head Gardener. At the first notes of the birds' song, he pushed his fingers into his ears and, as their song grew fuller and louder, he jumped out of bed, grumbling into his black beard.

'The wee rascals! I'll soon stop them! All that singing makes them hungry. Then they gobble up all the newly-planted rye seeds, which cost a lot of money – piles of silver sixpences.'

Hurriedly he dressed and grabbed his shot-gun. As he rushed into the garden, the birds flew off in great clouds into the trees.

BANG! went McFie's gun. BANG-BANG! None of the birds were hurt but the young ones were badly frightened by the noise. McFie shook his fist and shouted up at the trees,

'I'll catch you yet. You'll see.'

Later on that morning, a van drew up outside the Royal garden shed and from it were unloaded several large baskets.

'Good, very good,' said McFie, as he undid the fasteners on the baskets and out jumped . . . hundreds of CATS. Big ones, little ones, fat ones, thin ones, in fact, every kind you can think of. And soon, they were all prowling round the Palace Gardens. Now those cats had such hungry looks upon their faces and such sharp claws, that no bird dared to flutter down into the gardens, for the rest of that day.

That evening, from high up in the tree-tops the chorus of the birds was harsh.

'How dare he!' squawked the starlings.

'What shall we do, do,' cooed the pigeons.

'What chance have we against cruel teeth and claws?' cried the thrushes sadly.

'We'll fight with all our might,' sang the finches.

'War! War!' croaked all the crows.

'Let's peck off his whiskers,' shouted a cheeky sparrow.

'No! Listen to me!' sang sweet Jenny Wren. 'We'll fly to the Woodland to Mr Wonderful the magician. He'll know what to do.'

The birds flew up from the trees and away into the Woodland. Every nest was left empty. Every branch was left bare. Not one bird remained in the Palace Gardens.

At five o'clock the next morning, the King lay waiting for the sweet chorus to soothe him to sleep. But not a sound was to be heard. Six o'clock came. Then seven, still no birds sang.

'I can't understand it,' said the King, as he got out of bed at eight o'clock. 'The month of May, early morning and not a bird to be heard! What can the matter be?'

He was so upset he could not eat his breakfast. At last he wandered out into the gardens. And everywhere he went, he saw CATS. They were sitting in the flower beds, lazing on the lawns, sunning themselves on the terrace steps and dozing under the hedges.

'Where *have* they all come from? No wonder the birds are afraid to come into the gardens!'

He went back to the Palace and sent for Mr McFie at once.

'McFie,' said the King, 'why, are there so many cats in the Palace Gardens?'

'To protect your Royal plants and seeds, Your Majesty.'

'Nonsense,' said the King, 'the birds get rid of the pests. Besides, I like to hear them sing. So send those cats away at once and throw away that shot-gun of yours McFie. Then perhaps the birds will come back to my gardens.'

Mr McFie was very angry but he had to do as the King said, right away.

Now, away in the Woodland, Mr Wonderful was busy in his garden when the birds fluttered down to tell him their sad story. There were so many of them, the ground looked as if it was covered with a moving carpet of feathers.

Mr Wonderful listened very carefully then at last he said, 'All right. Then this is what you must do, tomorrow . . .' And he told them of his plan.

The next morning, at the Palace, after another sleepless night, the King felt tired and miserable. He was in his Counting House, trying to count out his money and his sum wouldn't come right at all.

Then a messenger came to tell him that an apple pie had been brought to the Palace. Now the King was very fond of apple pie and, as he had had no breakfast again, he was quite hungry. He hurried towards the dining room, calling to the Queen as he went,

'Apple pie for lunch today, my dear.'

'I hate apple pie,' replied the Queen, 'I shall have bread and honey in the parlour.'

'Very well, my darling,' said the King.

He sat down at the table, took up his knife and fork and lifted off the pastry crust. As he did so, out of the pie-dish popped a blackbird. Then another, and another . . . until there were four and twenty of them sitting around his plate. One of them held a folded paper in his beak which he placed before the King.

'Bless my soul,' exclaimed the King. He unfolded the paper written in Mr Wonderful's best writing, and read:

> 'Oh King we beseech you to grant our request,
> Let us return to the home we love best,
> You will sleep sweetly with dreams of delight,
> When the cats and the gun are banished from sight;
> There will be music sweet and clear,
> When the song of the birds is free from all fear.'

'Well, well,' said the King, 'I promise you the cats *have* been sent away and Mr McFie no longer has a gun. I haven't slept at all since you went away, so please come back and sing to me again.'

As soon as they heard this, the blackbirds flew at once to the Woodland to carry the good news to the others. All the birds returned to the Palace Gardens – each to his or her own particular tree and nest. The next morning they sang especially sweetly for the King to say thank you and how pleased they were to be home.

The Wonder House

One cold January morning the King and Queen were having breakfast. The King was trying to read his newspaper – the Queen was talking to him but he hadn't really been listening.

'Don't you agree?' she asked, tapping him sharply with her egg-spoon.

'Oh-ow-yes, of course, my dear,' mumbled the King, wondering what it was all about.

'Good! That's settled then.'

With a satisfied smile, she swept across the room and commanded one of the guards to fetch Mr Wonderful.

'Christmas is over. It must be someone's birthday,' thought the King, absent-mindedly putting his egg-spoon into the marmalade.

Mr Wonderful was usually only sent for to perform magic for Christmas and birthday parties now. Although once Mr Wonderful had performed wonderful and amazing magic, nowadays one could never be quite sure whether his magic would really work.

The King was still spooning marmalade into his egg and trying to remember whose birthday it was, when Mr Wonderful came in.

'About the party magic . . .' began the King vaguely.

'It was terrible!' interrupted the Queen. 'So bad in fact that someone else will perform Royal Magic from now on. He starts tomorrow. So you can pack your bags and go.'

'No!' exclaimed the King.

He liked Mr Wonderful and *he* was never tired of seeing the same old tricks. But Mr Wonderful was smiling.

17

'Oh yes please, Your Majesty! I find it difficult to do magic to order these days,' he said. 'Now I can spend all day doing the things I really enjoy. No more white rabbits, no more card tricks, no more . . .'

He stopped because the King looked sad.

'Don't go too far away old friend,' said the King. 'Perhaps on *my* birthdays you will still do magic tricks for me. And, in return for your long service, you may choose any place you wish to live in.'

Mr Wonderful hurried out of the room. 'I'd better start looking now for somewhere to live,' he thought.

So, he wrapped his cloak around him, put on his hat and walked out of the Palace grounds, up the hill towards the Woodland. The fields and hedgerows looked silvery and beautiful with their glittering covering of frost.

At the edge of the Woodland Mr Wonderful looked about him. Through the trees, he saw a black house. A light shone from a window and smoke curled from the chimney. Everything about the house was black – the window frames, the door and even the curtains. Mr Wonderful walked towards it, thinking he might peep through the windows to see who lived there.

The gate swung open with a loud 'SQUE . . . A . . . K'. Immediately the door of the house opened too. The biggest black cat he had ever seen came slowly down the path, rubbed its head against Mr Wonderful's legs, purring loudly.

'Sparks likes you, so you can come in,' said a voice.

Mr Wonderful looked up. Standing in the doorway was a strange old woman, dressed in black. She had long white hair, her face was wrinkled like a withered apple and her eyes were ice-blue.

'People call me Mrs Witch,' she said. 'I won't have anyone inside my cottage if my cat doesn't like them. So, come along in.'

Mr Wonderful followed her into the warm room. All round were shelves filled with old leather books, coloured bottles and strange prickly plants.

'Sit down,' she ordered. 'We'll have some tea, then you can tell me what brings you here.'

During tea, Mr Wonderful told Mrs Witch about his search for a new home. 'Perhaps,' he said, 'there's another cottage like this that I could live in.'

'No,' replied Mrs Witch. 'There's not another cottage like this anywhere. But I know of a place which might suit you. Come, I'll show you.'

High up under the tall trees was a rocky ledge. On this ledge was a huge old yellow car. It must have been the biggest car in the world and how it got on to that ledge was a complete mystery. Perhaps whoever had once owned the car, finding it was much too big to travel along any road, had dumped it there.

Now Mr Wonderful couldn't think of anything nicer than living in an old car. But the sun was setting behind the trees and he still had to collect his belongings from the Palace. He explained this to Mrs Witch.

'I'll help you,' said Mrs Witch. 'You fetch your things and I'll look around inside to see what has to be done.'

By the time Mr Wonderful returned, his nose was red with the cold. His hands were blue and as for his feet, he couldn't feel *them* at all. He stamped his feet to warm them. Each time he stamped, a peculiar 'BEEP-BEEP!' noise came from underneath his left foot. He prodded about in the frosty grass.

'Why!' he exclaimed, 'it's an old-fashioned motor horn! What a marvellous doorbell it will make for my new home.'

Mrs Witch called to him and once inside, Mr Wonderful could see how enormous the old car was. He pottered round making plans.

The driver's compartment would be his kitchen. All those rows of gadgets and shiny knobs on the dashboard would be very useful! The passenger part would make a comfortable living room and the boot, which had been built to take a ton of luggage, could be his bedroom.

Mrs Witch had been busy. The windows were clean, the floor polished, and she had made up a bed for him.

'How splendid!' said Mr Wonderful, 'and you've even put up black curtains for me.'

He thought it was a pity Mrs Witch didn't know much about colours.

'Well,' she demanded, 'what is *your* favourite colour?'

'Blue,' replied Mr Wonderful.

'As you wish,' she called, as she hurried back to her own house.

'What did she mean?' wondered Mr Wonderful. Then he saw that the curtains were now as blue as bluebells in spring.

Mr Wonderful felt so happy, and he said, 'I wonder what I can call my wonderful new house?'

Then, he smiled, 'That's it! It *is* wonderful. I'll call it – "The Wonder House".'

A Dog with a Waggly Tail

Mr Wonderful lived all alone in his car-house deep in the Woodland. His friend Mrs Witch sometimes visited him but often he felt rather lonely.

'Mrs Witch has her cat, Sparks, if only I had a pet too,' he sighed. 'What I would really like is a dog. A dog with a waggly tail.'

Now Mr Wonderful had no money to buy himself a dog, but he was clever at making things and suddenly he had a good idea.

For two whole days, he was busy hammering, sawing and fitting all kinds of bits together, until at last, he said,

'It's finished. My clockwork dog!'

Its coat was made of scraps of old blanket wool. It had two brown buttons for eyes and an old rope for its tail. Mr Wonderful even made a green wooden kennel for it – just like a real dog's. There were only two things wrong with it. It had to be wound up to make it walk, and it couldn't bark. Instead something inside the clockwork dog went 'I-am-a-dog; I-am-a-dog' every so often, in a funny growly voice.

It was such a fine afternoon Mr Wonderful thought he would call on Mrs Witch. He pulled on his hat and cloak, brushed the clockwork dog, wound it up, and off they went.

As they walked through the woodland, all kinds of creatures popped their heads out to have a look. One rabbit laughed so much when he saw the clockwork dog, his ears went wibbly-wobbly and he had hic-cups for the rest of the day. Another pretended to be very frightened and scampered away through the trees squeaking, 'Help! It says it's a dog!'

Now Sparks, who had been a witch's cat all his life, had never seen a dog before. He walked round the clockwork dog and patted it with his paw. He liked the wiggly-waggly tail, but every time it said 'I-am-a-dog', Sparks jumped with fright.

After Mr Wonderful had gone, Mrs Witch shook her head and sighed, 'It's not like a real dog, is it Sparks?'

Sparks couldn't answer because he didn't know what real dogs were like. But he thought to himself, 'I shall go and find a real live dog for Mr Wonderful tomorrow.'

Next morning it was pouring with rain. Sparks sat on the window-sill watching raindrops chasing one another down the window-panes. He longed for the rain to stop so that he could go off on his dog-search.

By afternoon the rain stopped – although the sky was full of black clouds. Sparks, picking his way round the puddles, set off down towards the village. He was just turning the corner into the High Street, when two huge animals came bounding towards him.

'Why, *they* must be dogs!'

Sparks ran towards them. No sooner did they see *him* than they leaped at him, barking and snapping. Sparks was so terrified he turned and ran. But, as he ran, other dogs appeared and joined in the chase.

Sparks raced on with the dogs close behind him. Then just ahead he saw a wall with the branches of a great tree hanging over it. Sparks jumped on to the wall and up into the branches. The dogs gathered around below, barking, snapping and yapping, but they could not reach him.

Sparks felt so frightened! He clung to the wet slippery branches. He was cold and hungry. It was getting dark too. He listened. It seemed very quiet now. The dogs must have gone away. He moved along the branch and on to the wall. But he didn't want to go back along the road again. Instead, he jumped down from the wall into a most untidy garden. He picked his way through the nettles and long grasses. Then . . . he got such a fright! His fur stood up on end like a spiky hedgehog!

There, in front of him, inside a tumble-down kennel and staring straight at him, was a dog. Sparks didn't know what to do. Then the dog spoke.

'Don't go, please! Stay and talk to me!'

His eyes looked so sad, Sparks asked, 'What's the matter?'

'The boy I belong to doesn't want me any more. He likes taking things to pieces and putting them together again. I'm sure he'd rather have a clockwork dog than a real one.'

'Is that so?' said Sparks, then his yellow eyes shone. 'I've just had a very good idea. Listen to me.'

Hurriedly he whispered his plan to the little dog. Then, very quietly, they both crept through the garden under the gate and into the back lane. They glanced up at the house. All was quiet. They hurried on towards Mr Wonderful's house in the Woodland.

Mr Wonderful had already gone to bed. He had left his clockwork dog in the toolshed. The brown dog laughed when he saw the clockwork dog. The rain had made it rather rusty and Mr Wonderful was going to oil and grease it the next day.

'How can we get him back to my kennel?' whispered the dog. 'We can't wind him up, he's so rusty he'd make too much noise.'

'We'll drag him along between us,' hissed Sparks.

It took a long time to get the clockwork dog to the brown dog's kennel. The two weary animals returned to the Woodland just as the last stars were fading from the sky.

'I'd love to see Mr Wonderful's face in the morning when he finds you,' yawned Sparks, 'but I must go home now. Goodnight!'

Mr Wonderful was delighted when, instead of a rusty clockwork dog, he found a real live dog. A dog with warm brown fur and a waggly tail. Mr Wonderful couldn't think how such a wonderful thing had happened.

The boy was pleased too to find he had a new toy he could take to pieces and put together again.

As for Sparks and the brown dog, they became great friends. For they shared a very special secret, didn't they?

The Little Dog Laughed

Mr Wonderful couldn't understand it at all. Toby, his dog, was very unhappy and wouldn't eat his food. Mr Wonderful had made him a very special dish too. He had made the dish out of an old saucepan lid he'd found in the hedge. He had fitted legs underneath it so that the dish could move. It could come all by itself to be filled with food and then take it back to Toby's special corner of the kitchen.

Now that dish was the cause of all the trouble, although Mr Wonderful didn't know it. It was a very naughty dish; perhaps it had been a naughty saucepan lid and that was why it had been thrown away. Anyway, it made poor Toby very miserable. Whenever he went to eat from it, the dish would start to whisper nasty things in Toby's ears. So Toby would wander off into a corner and lie there with his head on his paws looking sad.

'I'll go and ask Mrs Witch what she thinks would make Toby happy again' Mr Wonderful decided.

Now Mrs Witch's cat Sparks was a most unusual cat. Shall I tell you why? He could play the fiddle so enchantingly that even worms would dance to his music. Toby and Sparks were great friends, and while they played in the garden, Mr Wonderful and Mrs Witch talked together.

'I know,' said Mrs Witch at last. 'Let's have a Sports Day. It'll do everyone good. Now it's springtime it'll help all those sleepy creatures to wake up after their winter sleep.'

So it was arranged. A notice was put up on a tree in the middle of the Woodland:

SPORTS DAY
Saturday

*Hopping, jumping, or running races
for two legs, three, four or more.
A special prize for the winner.*

Soon every creature in the Woodland was practising for the great day. Breathless 'Ready-steady-go's could be heard everywhere. The air was full of scurryings and flurryings.

Meanwhile, Mr Wonderful was in his kitchen searching through all his cupboards for a special cup to give to the winner.

'China, chipped too, that won't do!' he murmured, rummaging about the shelves, 'It should be silver. This tin one won't do either. Oh dear! I'll have to think of something else, that's all.'

He wandered out into the sunshine down to the bluebell dell. There were bluebells everywhere and clusters of

primroses under the trees. And, in amongst the primroses, something glittered and twinkled up at him.

'What can it be?' he said. He bent down and picked up a beautiful silver spoon with the letter 'W' engraved on its handle.

'What could be better!' he exclaimed and he put the spoon carefully into his pocket. 'A silver spoon instead of a silver cup as a prize! And it has "W" for winner already on it.'

As Mr Wonderful turned back home, Daisy, the Fresian cow, grazing in the meadow stuck her head over the hedge and mooed,

'May I be in the Sports too?'

Mr Wonderful hesitated. Daisy was rather large.

'Watch me jump high,' called Daisy.

She raced off down the meadow, and leapt high in the air. Even the lambs across on the far hills watched her.

'Well done,' congratulated Mr Wonderful. 'Keep practising. We'll all come down here to the meadow to see you jump on Saturday.'

This made Daisy very happy. Mr Wonderful was happy too. He went home and polished the spoon until it shone like a star. That bad dish was watching him.

'By hook or by crook,' it said to itself, 'I'll steal that spoon.' And it began to work out a wicked plan.

Saturday came at last. All the little creatures lined up ready and waiting. Mr Wonderful gave the signal for the races to start. Mrs Witch was at the winning post

to see who came in first. Toby trotted up and down barking encouragement to the stragglers. Sparks played his fiddle to help them run faster.

Now, back at Mr Wonderful's house, that bad dish had been left on the kitchen table with the silver spoon. The dish edged closer to the spoon.

'Oh spoon,' he cooed, 'how beautiful you are.'

'Yes, I know I am,' drawled the spoon.

'Much too fine and elegant to be given away to some common little creature who wouldn't know how to use you properly,' said he.

'Oh yes indeed,' shuddered the spoon, 'I'm much too good for that!'

'Then run away with me, lovely spoon.'

'Yes, let's go now,' squeaked the spoon peevishly, 'I won't stay here another minute. But oh – how can I, I haven't got legs like you?'

'Don't worry,' said the dish, 'I'll carry you off to the most wonderful places.'

Little did that silly spoon guess they would get no further than the first shop-keeper who would buy her.

Just at that moment Daisy was jumping as she had never jumped before. Sparks played a tune upon his fiddle. Up and up and up went Daisy.

'She's jumped over the moon!' squeaked an excited mouse.

All eyes were fixed on Daisy so that no one saw that bad dish as he ran away with the spoon – except Toby and he laughed and laughed.

Mr Wonderful was pleased Toby was happy again. He had quite forgotten about the prize spoon. So had everyone else. Nobody really minded who won.

'Let's have a Sports Day every year,' chorused hundreds of happy voices.

'I'll play one last tune before we all go to bed,' said Sparks.

You can probably guess what it was . . .
Hey diddle diddle, the cat and the fiddle,
The cow jumped over the moon,
The little dog laughed to see such fun,
And the dish ran away with the spoon.

A Very Strange Noise

Horace Hedgehog had just settled down for his winter's sleep when there was a banging at the door.

'Rat-a-tat! Rat-a-tat.'

'Oh go away,' he mumbled, snuggling closer into the warm bedclothes.

'Rat-a-tat-bang. Rat-a-tat-BANG!'

This time it was so loud that he nearly fell out of bed.

'I'm coming,' he called crossly.

He shuffled down the dark passage, drew back the heavy bolts on the door. When he opened it, there stood a most extraordinary creature. It had legs and feet, wings and a tail like his friend Tommy Thrush, but its head was just like a donkey's.

'Let me in, please Horace,' said the strange-looking creature, 'I'm so cold and hungry. I can't go home like this. My mother wouldn't know it was me.'

Horace Hedgehog knew that voice.

'Why Tommy Thrush,' he said, 'what are you doing with that silly thing on your head. Take it off at once.'

'That's just it,' Tommy replied tearfully, 'I can't. I'm too heavy to fly now with a big head like this and I don't suppose I shall ever sleep in a nest again.'

'Now, don't cry,' said Horace, 'you'd better come inside. Then we'll see what can be done.'

Tommy struggled along the narrow passage as best he could. Horace had to give him a push every now and then to keep him from getting stuck.

'Well,' began Tommy, when they at last reached Horace's sittingroom, 'this morning, I hopped on to Mrs Witch's window-sill to see what kind of spells she was making. There was a lot of green smoke in the room, so I thought I'd play a trick on her. I called out "Fire! Fire! Something's burning." I suppose it gave her a fright, because she jumped round, knocking the pan off the stove and everything was spilt. She *was* angry. She threw some magic at me, and well, you can see what happened. What can I do Horace? I must have my own head back. This one's so heavy and it makes horrible noises when I sing. Listen.'

Horace, who had been getting sleepier and sleepier was rudely awakened by the noise.

'Br-a-a-h, br-a-a-h.'

'Yes,' said Horace firmly, 'we'll have to put a stop to that, otherwise none of us will ever get any sleep again. Well, as it was put there by magic, we must get some more magic to take it away. Wait a minute, I'll see if there's any in the kitchen cupboard.'

He padded off down the passage into his neat kitchen. Tommy could hear the chink-chink of bottles being moved and rearranged on the shelves and little muttery noises as Horace sleepily mumbled to himself.

'Ah-ha!' he heard Horace say. Then more loudly, 'Just the thing!'

'Have you found something?' he called eagerly.

'Not quite,' said Horace, who had reappeared in the sitting-room surprisingly quickly, looking wide-awake now and holding a blue bottle in his paw, 'But I have found something else which will be useful.'

Tommy looked at the label on the bottle. It said 'Magic for keeping hedgehogs awake in winter' and then underneath in smaller letters, 'Mr Wonderful, Wonder House, Woodland.'

'You could try some of this if you like Tommy. I've just had some. It tastes like strawberries and sunshine, all mixed up.'

'I don't think I should,' said Tommy. 'After all, I'm a thrush not a hedgehog, so it won't do at all.'

'You're probably right,' answered Horace, 'but I have a better idea. We'll go and see Mr Wonderful and get the proper kind of magic for you.'

Tommy felt so much happier, he nearly tried to sing again, but Horace quickly put a paw over his mouth and said,

'Not now, it'll sound better when you get your old head back again.'

Horace brushed his bristles, put on his cap and scarf and off they went. It was very cold and the fallen leaves rustled and crackled beneath their feet. Horace thought longingly of his comfortable bed. But his friend was in trouble and he must help him first.

Mr Wonderful's house was a strange and exciting place, made out of an old car which someone had dumped in the woods long ago. The horn of the old car was now a doorbell with a notice underneath which read,

'Hoot twice, loud and clear. Come in. Wipe your feet on the mat, please.'

Horace carefully pressed the horn twice and immediately the door was flung open. He and Tommy had only just enough time to get inside when the door closed again all by itself. They looked round and saw Mr Wonderful coming towards them. As he saw Tommy, Mr Wonderful started to laugh.

'Please don't laugh at him,' said Horace hurriedly, 'he doesn't think it is at all funny.'

And he went on to explain what had happened to Tommy.

Mr Wonderful rubbed his chin thoughtfully and then he said,

'You don't really need magic to put that right! All you have to do is go to Mrs Witch and tell her that you're sorry. Or, better still, sing it,' he added with a mischievous smile.

'Oh thank you, Mr Wonderful,' said Tommy. 'Why didn't I think of that before?'

Off he and Horace went, until they came to Mrs Witch's house. Tommy hesitated by the gate.

'You'd better stay here, just in case she turns you into something else,' he whispered to Horace. 'And supposing she won't change me back?'

'She will!' said Horace firmly and gave his friend a little push. Tommy's donkey nose knocked against the bell. The door opened and there stood Mrs Witch, looking rather grim.

'What is it?' she snapped.

'Please,' began Tommy, haltingly, 'I've come to say I'm sorry for spoiling your spell and . . .'

But Mrs Witch was laughing and tears were rolling down her cheeks.

'Oh dear,' she gasped, 'I haven't seen anything quite so funny for a long time. Did I really do that to you?'

Tommy suddenly remembered what Mr Wonderful had said about singing to her. So, he opened his mouth and brayed in his loudest voice,

'If you like this song,
I can sing all night long;
But it would sound sweeter,
If my head were much neater.'

'Yes *indeed*,' said Mrs Witch clamping her hands over her ears. Then quickly taking a magic spell from her store cupboard she sprinkled it three times over Tommy's head and gabbled 'Abracadabracandelabra.'

Immediately, Tommy was a real thrush again and he was so happy, he started to sing in great sweet bursts of song.

'That's really beautiful Tommy. I like you much better like that,' said Mrs Witch. 'Come and sing to me again in the morning. I can see Horace Hedgehog at the gate and, by the look of him, he should be sleeping his winter sleep now. So off you go.'

'Thank you, thank you,' sang Tommy, as he hopped along beside his friend Horace, who was almost walking in his sleep by now.

Horace was glad to get back home again. He fell asleep at once. And his dreams were filled with happy thoughts of warm spring days to come, of pale yellow sunlight, fresh green leaves and birds sweetly singing.

A Very Rare Animal

In the early months of spring, round the hollow tree in the meadow, Rufus Fox and his sisters and brothers played happily together. They hadn't a care in the world. But, when autumn came, the huntsmen in bright red coats set out on horseback with their hounds to catch the foxes.

All the foxes hid themselves away very cunningly. All except Rufus, who was not so clever. He ran hither and thither to escape from the huntsmen.

At last, there, just ahead of him was Mr Wonderful's yellow car-house. The door was open and Rufus dashed straight in.

Now, just at that moment Mr Wonderful was standing on a chair painting his kitchen ceiling with some special blue and white paint which he had just invented. As Rufus rushed in, down came

Mr Wonderful and 'sloosh' went the paint all over the fox. Rufus was so frightened, he hardly noticed at all.

'Save me,' he begged. '*Please* hide me.'

'Gracious me,' said Mr Wonderful, as he picked himself up from the floor and looked at the blue and white fox, 'if you could only see yourself! You don't look a bit like a fox now. Except for your beautiful golden tail.'

'Then,' pleaded Rufus, 'cut some of the fur off my tail so they won't recognize me.'

Outside the shouting and the horn-blowing came nearer and nearer.

'Quickly, please,' said Rufus.

'All right,' agreed Mr Wonderful.

'Snip snip' went his scissors, and he had only just finished when in rushed a crowd of hot-faced huntsmen shouting,

'The fox! Where's the fox?'

'Fox?' said Mr Wonderful, 'Um . . . have you lost a fox, gentlemen?'

Down at his feet was a shivering blue and white spotted animal with a long stringy tail.

'Egad! What's that?' asked one man, pointing at poor trembling Rufus.

'That? oh . . . it's a . . . um . . . very rare animal,' said Mr Wonderful, trying hard to think what kind of name an animal looking like that would have.

'Yes, I can see that!' snapped the Queen, who had just come in. 'But *what is it called?*'

'It's a woxy, Your Majesty,' said Mr Wonderful. 'There isn't another one like it in the world.'

'Then I must have him for my zoo. He shall live in a golden cage and eat only the finest grapes and honey. My men shall take him back to the Palace at once.'

Mr Wonderful opened his mouth, then closed it again. It was not wise to argue with the Queen.

'Don't worry,' he whispered to Rufus, 'I'll think of a way to get you out.'

But Rufus was rather pleased at the thought of living in the Queen's zoo and feeding on grapes and honey. That would be much better than being chased all over the countryside.

A few days went by. Mr Wonderful had finished painting his kitchen and he suddenly remembered about Rufus. But when he reached the zoo, what a sorry sight met his eyes! In the corner of a golden cage lay a very unhappy blue and white spotted animal with a stringy tail. None of the other visitors gave him a second glance. They hurried off to see the penguins, to laugh at the monkeys and to watch the sea-lions being fed.

'Rufus,' whispered Mr Wonderful. 'What's the matter old fellow?'

'I'm so unhappy,' cried Rufus, 'I don't like it here. I don't like honey and grapes any more. They make me sick. I'm homesick!'

Mr Wonderful thought for a moment then he said, 'Stand up Rufus. Aha! Just as I thought! You're as thin as a shadow, only shadows aren't blue and white.'

'How clever of you to notice,' sneered Rufus. He was feeling *so* miserable, he wanted to make someone else miserable too.

'Now listen to me,' said Mr Wonderful, 'I've thought of a wonderful plan. Come here and I'll tell you.'

As Mr Wonderful whispered his plan, a sly gleam came into Rufus's yellow eyes and he grinned from ear to ear.

That afternoon, Mr Wonderful went home and swept all his carpets. He soon collected a great pile of black dust which he shook carefully into a bag. Then, taking the bag with him he hurried off again to the zoo.

It was just before closing time. He went straight to the woxy's cage. Glancing all around to make sure nobody was looking, he pushed the bag through the bars of the cage.

'Good luck, Rufus,' he whispered and hurried out of the gate, just as the keepers were locking up for the night.

Darkness came and most of the animals settled down to sleep. But Rufus very stealthily undid the bag which Mr Wonderful had brought him and sprinkled the dust over the floor of his cage. He covered himself with honey from his golden dish, then he rolled over and over in the dust until he was no longer blue and white, but a dark dusty colour. Then, like a thin dark shadow of the night, he slipped through the bars of his cage, crept down the long path and out under the Visitors' Gate and no one noticed him at all.

Then away he ran and ran, until he was once more safely under the old hollow tree in the meadow. There he stayed hidden for a long time until his fur and tail were once more goldenly beautiful again.

The next day, the Queen was told that the woxy had completely vanished. She was very puzzled and angry.

'Send for Mr Wonderful!' she commanded.

Mr Wonderful appeared before her and bowed low.

'Mr Wonderful,' she said, 'my woxy has completely disappeared. No one seems to know why. Can *you* give me an explanation.'

'Oh yes,' replied Mr Wonderful, 'that's the way with woxys. Here one minute, gone the next. Sometimes they just vanish into thin air. That is why, Your Majesty, they are such rare animals.'

The King's New Rose

It was a beautiful morning. Just the kind of morning when the sun and the birds call everyone to come out of doors and enjoy themselves. But no one at the Palace was out of doors. They were all *very* worried – most of all the Lord Chamberlain. When he was opening the morning Palace post, amongst the letters was a very grubby postcard which made him frown and exclaim

'No one would dare!'

Printed on the postcard in large letters was a message which read:

He walked along the corridor towards the breakfast-room and met the Queen, who was also carrying a postcard and looking very angry indeed.

'Lord Chamberlain,' she said in icy tones, 'something must be done about this. There are times,' she went on, as she suddenly caught sight of the King wandering down to breakfast in his pyjamas, 'when *I* don't like the King either – why *doesn't* he get dressed earlier in the morning! But that is no reason to kidnap him and you, Lord Chamberlain, must put a stop to it.'

'Yes, Your Majesty,' said the Lord Chamberlain meekly, and hurried off to telephone the Chief of Police and all the Chiefs of all the King's Armed Forces.

The King had received a postcard too. But he hadn't bothered about it. He'd just torn it up and thrown it in the waste-paper basket. When he had finished his breakfast (and *finally* got dressed) he decided to take a walk to the Royal Woods. It was so peaceful there and he wouldn't be disturbed by the Queen, who did *not* like walking. He was just about to go through the great golden gates when the Queen called in her most terrible voice:

'Jonathan, where do you think you are going?'

As he turned round to answer her, two guards appeared almost by magic; they closed the gates with a harsh clang.

'Don't you know you can't go outside the grounds until the Lord Chamberlain has discovered who is sending these unpleasant threats?' she demanded.

'Oh, fiddlesticks,' said the King crossly. 'If she had her way,' he thought, 'I'd never have *any* fun.'

Then he decided to go to the Royal Lake and sit by the willow tree to watch the fishes swimming in the clear, glittering waters, and if he sat very still, he might even see a kingfisher skim over the Lake. But the waters were rippled and troubled today and he had no sooner seated himself under the willow tree, when out of the Lake popped the periscope of a submarine, with the royal coat-of-arms on it.

'Oh botheration!' exclaimed the King. Even the Royal Navy had been called in for his protection – and to spoil his day!

He stood thinking and wondering where he could go to be right away from ever-watchful eyes.

'Ah, yes, just the place!' he thought and set off in the direction of the Royal Maze. Even if a guard were sent in to follow him, the King knew he could soon lose him, so complicated was the plan of the Maze that only the King himself knew by heart the best paths to follow to get right to the centre and the ones to take to get out again.

The King was very pleased to see that there was no guard on duty at the entrance to the Maze, so no one would follow him in. But, he was wrong. As he hurried down the narrow leafy paths he thought he heard soft creeping footsteps behind him. He turned his head quickly but could see no one and yet . . . surely the leaves just there were moving slightly, as if someone had brushed against them? Feeling somewhat uneasy, he continued on his way to the centre of the Maze and there a very unpleasant surprise awaited him.

Standing by the sundial in the very centre was black-bearded Mr McFie, the King's Head Gardener. The King never had liked Mr McFie, or his big black beard and today the King thought he looked even more unpleasant.

'I'm sure you received my postcard this morning,' said McFie with a sinister smile.

'Oh, so it was you,' replied the King. Then he noticed McFie was holding a huge brown sack in his hands.

'I'm a very patient man, Your Majesty. I guessed you'd come into the Maze sooner or later. It wasn't easy to find my way to the centre, but it was easy to get rid of the guard at the entrance, I sent him away on an errand. And,' he went on, with a nasty chuckle, 'I have only to put you in this sack to get you right away

from the Palace. Nobody will ever suspect *me* of the kidnapping. It won't be a bit of good for you to call for help. There's no one within earshot for miles.'

What happened next took place all so quickly that the King and McFie were both taken by surprise. McFie was just about to throw the sack over the King's head, when someone knocked him smartly on the head from behind, snatched the sack from his grubby hands and pushed *him* into it and tied the string. When the King recovered from his surprise, he saw the newcomer was Peter, the boy who worked in the Royal Kitchen Gardens.

'Peter,' said the King, shaking him warmly by the hand, 'I've never been more pleased to see anyone in all my life. But just what are you doing here, and how did you discover the way through the Maze?'

'Well,' said Peter, blushing and looking rather uncomfortable, 'I don't really like working in the Kitchen Gardens. I don't like looking after cabbages and cauliflowers although Mr McFie made me. What I really want to do is to grow roses and . . . I have made a secret garden here by the sundial. I'm sorry, Your Majesty, I knew I shouldn't have done it.'

'Sorry!' echoed the King in astonishment, as he knelt down to pick one of the red roses which was growing on a bush in the newly-made flower bed. 'This is the most beautiful of all the flowers in the Royal Gardens.'

He placed the tiny flower carefully into his buttonhole. In the Palace gardens there were roses as large as cabbages with petals softer than silk but, to the King, this rose in his buttonhole was finer than them all, and its perfume was unusually sweet.

It took the King and Peter a long time to drag that heavy sack with the huge McFie, out of the Maze and it was nearly noon when they reached the Palace.

At the door of the Palace stood a crowd of people. The Queen still looked grim. The Lord Chamberlain looked very pleased with himself, and so did the Chief of Police.

'You're late!' snapped the Queen.

'Your Majesty, we've discovered who's been sending the threatening notes,' said the Lord Chamberlain and the Chief of Police, together. 'His fingerprints are on all the cards. His name is . . .'

'. . . McFie. I know,' interrupted the King, 'you'll find him in this sack. And I,' he went on happily, 'have found a new Head Gardener and his name is *Peter*.'

And with that, humming a happy tune to himself, the King walked into the Palace to have his lunch.

Little Green Frog

In the middle of the lake in Tall Trees Park is Frog Island. In springtime, when golden kingcups are in flower there, the frogs return after their long winter sleep. On fine evenings, the old frogs croak songs of long ago. The young frogs sing too, of the days to come and the wonderful things they will do. And they play leap-frog by the light of the moon.

'I can jump high, higher than anyone,' sang the youngest and bravest little green frog.

'All right, let's see you jump over that fallen tree-trunk,' chorused the old frogs.

The moon shone down upon the little frog's handsome green coat and sparkled in his big black eyes.

Little green frog took a deep breath, puffed out his chest and with a one-two-three, he jumped right over the tree-trunk and landed in the soft springy grass by the water's edge.

A grass snake was lazing in the water, gently swaying itself back and forth.

'Where did you come from?' he murmured, opening one eye.

'I've just jumped over that great tree-trunk, didn't you see me?' asked the little green frog.

'No-oo!' hissed the snake, opening both eyes very wide and thinking to himself what a delicious dinner that fine fat frog would make for a snake. 'But I *would* like to see you jump again. Ple-ease jump on to that water-lily leaf over there.'

Little green frog took a deep breath, puffed out his chest and with a one-two-three, he jumped over the water-lily leaf, across the water, right over to the other side of the lake.

'Shuddering sausage-skins! My dinner's got away,' hissed the snake, swishing himself backwards and forwards in a rage.

But little green frog didn't hear him. He had landed on the path which runs underneath the willow trees right beside a tabby-cat out for her evening prowl. She arched her back, spread her claws and spat at him.

'Where did you come from? You did give me a fright!' she complained.

'I've jumped over a tree-trunk and over the lake and I can jump even higher if I try,' said the brave little frog proudly.

'Well, just jump over that larch tree,' purred the cat sweetly, thinking to herself, 'He'll get stuck on the top branches and that'll serve him right for scaring me.'

And she began to clean her silver whiskers with her paws.

So, little green frog took a deep breath, puffed out his chest and with a one-two-three, he jumped right over the larch tree and landed among the buttercups in a field where a black-and-white cow was grazing.

'Where did you come from?' mooed the cow in great surprise, 'You weren't there a minute ago.'

'I've jumped over a tree-trunk, over the lake and over that tall larch tree. I can jump even higher if I try,' declared the frog. His legs were aching by now and he was really very tired, but he wasn't going to say so.

'Humph!' said the cow. 'That's nothing. Nothing at all. My granny once told me a story about a cow who jumped right over the moon, and I don't suppose *you* could do that.'

'Oh yes I can,' answered the frog, 'you just watch me.'

By now he was so weary he would much rather have crept under a large stone and fallen asleep.

He took a deep breath, puffed out his chest and with a one-two-three, he jumped, up into the sky. But the cow didn't even lift her head.

'Humph!' she said, as she chewed another mouthful of sweet young grass. 'He'll get lost in space. That's what happens to those who can't keep their feet on the ground.'

Higher and higher went the little green frog. Over the clouds and on and on he went. Over the moon and then he landed, BUMP, upon a rain cloud.

'Well, well, little frog,' said the rain cloud, 'where did you come from?'

'I've jumped over a tree-trunk, over the lake, over the tall larch tree in the Park and over the moon,' replied the frog. 'But I would like to go home now.'

'Well done frog!' replied the rain cloud. 'Now, I am sending the rain down to earth. Shall I send you back there too?'

'Yes please,' murmured the frog, sleepily. 'I am glad I've had so many adventures,' he said, as he sped back down to earth, 'because I know now, I can do anything – if I try hard enough.'

Halloween Magic

There was once a witch called Fenella. Now Fenella was very unhappy. She really wasn't much good as a witch and, to make matters even worse, her two sisters were such wonderful witches.

They couldn't understand it at all.

'How can you be so stupid!' they said. 'You can't even mix a magic spell without getting lumps in it.'

'I know,' said Fenella miserably, 'I can't do any magic properly. I'm useless.'

'I'll just have to go on trying,' she sighed, putting all the wrong things into her magic cauldron. It was *supposed* to be a spell for the King to charm a pimple off the end of his nose, but the spell Fenella made charmed off the King's nose and left the pimple! Her two sisters quickly put it right again, but the King was *very* cross and Fenella felt more unhappy than ever.

Now when Halloween's night came, the King gave a party. Fenella's sisters were invited but the King hadn't quite forgiven Fenella for the muddle over his nose, so she wasn't asked.

'I don't mind,' she sniffed, as she listened to the wind howling round the roof-tops and rattling at the windows. 'It's much nicer to stay at home on a night like this.'

But she did feel a tiny bit miserable as she watched her sisters going off, all a-sparkle and a-spangle in their best party clothes.

'I know,' she said suddenly, 'I'll make a fine-weather spell, that's sure to please everyone. And I'll make some gingerbread, just to cheer myself up.'

After she had popped the gingerbread into the oven, she began the fine-weather spell, mixing 'a-little-bit-of-this' and 'a-little-bit-of-that', singing and dancing all the while, because she felt happier now. As she danced round the cauldron for the third time, there was a flash and a mighty gust of wind blew the door open.

In through the open door sailed a big umbrella and underneath it the roundest jolliest little lady Fenella had ever seen.

'A-a-are you my fairy godmother?' asked Fenella.

'Bless you, no, child. Witches don't have fairy godmothers! I'm your Great Aunt Rattleprattle, and you sent for me, didn't you? What's the trouble?'

She had to shout very loudly, to be heard over the noise of the wind.

'Oh dear!' cried Fenella, sitting down suddenly. 'My sisters are right. I'm not fit to be a witch! That was supposed to be a fine-weather spell.'

Through her tears, Fenella told Great Aunt Rattleprattle all her troubles.

'Now, now my dear,' laughed Great Aunt Rattleprattle, 'it may not have been quite right for a fine-weather spell, but it did bring me here and I'm going to help you. First of all, I'll stop that wind, I can't hear myself think!'

She unscrewed the handle of her umbrella, took out a small blue bottle labelled 'Pong of pongs', sprinkled it into the cauldron, clapped her hands three times and the wind died down at once.

'Now bring me your book of spells, Fenella dear, and I'll see where it is you go wrong,' said Great Aunt Rattleprattle.

'Yes Aunt,' replied Fenella, 'and I'll go and see if the gingerbread is done.'

It didn't take Great Aunt Rattleprattle long to see that Fenella's spells were quite hopeless.

'Well, Aunt?' asked Fenella, coming in with a tray of rich golden-brown gingerbread.

'Well, I think . . .' began Great Aunt Rattleprattle, absent-mindedly taking a piece of gingerbread and biting into it, 'I think . . . my dear, this is delicious! Did *you* make this?'

'Yes' said Fenella.

'Can your sisters cook like this too?'

'Oh no!' replied Fenella. 'They can't even make toast without burning it.'

'Well then,' laughed Great Aunt Rattleprattle, 'you don't need to bother about magic. Keep to the things you do best. Let them do the magic. You do the cooking.'

'Thank you Aunt, I will,' said Fenella, kissing her and throwing her spellbook away, whereupon Great Aunt Rattleprattle disappeared in a flash back to her home.

Fenella has never made a magic spell since that day. But her cooking – ah yes, that's quite a different story! Lots of people now enjoy her delicious gingerbread, especially the King, who invites Fenella to all his parties now, even when it isn't Halloween.

A Witch's Cat

None of the animals stayed long in Mr Fry's pet shop. They were soon bought by pet-lovers. All except Sooty. Mr Fry was very disappointed over him. Sooty was just an ordinary black cat, who had come to the shop in a basket with four brothers and sisters. They had been sold quickly, but not Sooty.

'There must be someone who wants a little cat like you,' Mr Fry would say to Sooty.

But Sooty did not want to be just anybody's cat. Oh no! Sooty wanted to be a witch's cat.

Now, one afternoon, just as Mr Fry was about to hang up the 'Closed' sign on the door, a very witchy-looking lady, carrying a basket, came into the shop.

'I must have a black cat at once,' she said.

She looked all round the shop and then she saw Sooty.

'I'll take that one,' she said, pointing to Sooty.

Sooty was pleased. He was quite sure she was a witch.

When the lady got home, she opened her basket and took Sooty out. He looked about him. It was just as he had imagined a witch's kitchen would be.

'Now pay attention,' snapped the lady. 'I'm a witch and you're going to work for me. And don't ever try to run away like the last ones did.'

'Oh no, I won't,' said Sooty, quickly. 'I've always wanted to be a witch's cat. Really I have.'

'Good,' replied the witch, 'then get started. You can clean the floors, wash-up the dishes, weed the garden and then . . .'

She took down from the shelf three large and dusty books,

'. . . get these three spells done before I get back. I'm going out for an hour.'

Sooty watched her from the window, as she went down the path. An hour was not long and he wondered how he would get everything done in that time. So he decided to start with the spells.

'Spell No. 72,' he read,' "To make people miserable" – what a nasty idea! I don't want to do that! What's the next one?'

The next one was no better either – 'To make sick people sicker'.

'Ugh!' said Sooty, feeling quite sick himself. The last one was Spell No. 99.

'I wonder what that one's for?' he said. 'Something horrible, I expect.'

But Sooty was a brave cat and a clever cat. And he had an idea.

'I know!' he said, 'I'll make all the spells backwards, then they can't cause any harm.'

He wondered what he would do if the witch came home before he had finished making the back-to-front spells. She would be back at one o'clock and already the hands of the kitchen clock were pointing to half-past twelve.

Then Sooty noticed for the first time a whole row of wooden black cats in a semicircle round the fire. His paws must have been a bit shaky, because Spell No. 99, which he had just finished mixing, fell to the floor with a crash and spilled all over the place.

'I'm not *really* afraid of that witch,' he said aloud to make himself feel better.

'And we're not afraid of her now,' mewed a great chorus of cat voices, 'we'll help you.'

Sooty jumped round in surprise. The back-to-front spell had splashed over the wooden cats and they had become real cats again.

'Come on then,' cried Sooty, feeling quite brave now. 'We'll mix all her spells backwards, so that her magic will be undone.'

The cats worked like lightning. Only one spell was left to be back-to-fronted when the witch came up the path.

'Quick!' called Sooty. 'All together – mix the last spell.'

The door was just opening, any moment the witch would be inside the house. Suddenly, as all the cats together stirred the last spell, there was a BANG and a puff of green smoke. And, when the smoke had cleared away, and the cats looked about them, the witch's house had vanished, so had the witch and – she's never been seen since.

Sooty took the other cats with him to Mr Fry, who looked after them until they were sold to good homes. And Sooty? Well, he certainly did not want to be a witch's cat, after that. Somebody bought him. Perhaps you've got a black cat called Sooty, have you?

The Higgledy-Piggledy House

Down upon the sea-shore there was once a house. And what a funny house it was. It was all higgledy-piggledy.

'No matter how hard I try,' said the house, 'I can't stand up straight.'

Its windows sloped this way. Its doors sloped that way. Its ceilings were all sagging and its floors weren't flat.

Now on sunny days the higgledy-piggledy house was happy. Children came down to the sea-shore. They came over the red rugged cliffs. They had picnics and played on the smooth sand. Sometimes they paddled in and out of the sea.

But when it was cold and wintry,
when the wind blew,
when the sky was grey and the sea was inky black, no children came.

No one came anywhere near the higgledy-piggledy house except the grey sea-gull. He always stopped to rest on the higgledy-piggledy chimneys whenever he was flying that way. He told the higgledy-piggledy house stories about the other houses in the country and the town.

He was there one misty-moisty morning when he heard the higgledy-piggledy house cry,
'Ooh I am so sad.'

Great black sooty tears ran down the chimneys.

'I'm all alone!' sobbed the higgledy-piggledy house. 'No one loves me.'

'Well I love you,' squawked the sea-gull, 'I like the way your windows slope this way and your doors slope that way, your ceilings all sagging and your floors that aren't flat. And there must be lots of people who would love a higgledy-piggledy house like you.'

But the higgledy-piggledy house went on crying. So the sea-gull said,

'Now listen, you're no ordinary house. You're a higgledy-piggledy house. I'm sure a house like you can do anything at all you want to do.'

The higgledy-piggledy house straightened up a bit, thought for a moment and said,

'Then I'd like to move. I'd like to go to some of the places you've been. That's what I'd like to do.'

'Today's the day,' called the sea-gull. 'There's a swirly-curly fog coming in from the sea. It's just the day for magic and mystery.'

The swirly-curly fog was spreading all over the sea-shore, and all over the red rugged cliffs. The higgledy-piggledy house pulled itself up as straight and as tall as it could and off it went. Up over the cliff tops. Away down the long steep road between the hedges, almost hidden in the swirly-curly fog.

After a while, quite a long while, the higgledy-piggledy house found itself in front of some very grand iron gates. The higgledy-piggledy house blinked through its windows. It stared through the swirly-curly fog. Beyond the gates was a smooth white drive and on each side were flowers of all colours.

'Ooooh,' sighed the higgledy-piggledy

house, 'this is the place for me. I'll stay here.'

The higgledy-piggledy house was tired after travelling such a long way. There were blisters on its humpy-bumpy floorboards and its sagging ceilings ached.

'Yes, this is where I'll stay,' yawned the higgledy-piggledy house and settled down to rest right in the middle of the drive.

Now, it wasn't very long before the rich man, whose drive it was, came home. And, when his golden car nearly crashed into the higgledy-piggledy house in the swirly-curly fog, the rich man was very angry indeed.

'What's that higgledy-piggledy heap of bricks doing in my drive,' he roared. 'Clear it away at once.'

So, the higgledy-piggledy house set off at once to find another place to stay.

Over the fields, through the long cool grasses, the higgledy-piggledy house went until it came to a farmyard. Horses, cows, pigs and hens lived there.

'Oh I shall like it here,' said the higgledy-piggledy house. 'This is where I'll stay.'

But, oh dear, as soon as the animals saw the higgledy-piggledy house in the middle of their farmyard, they all began to shout and snort, to squawk and squeal.

'This is our farmyard. You're in the way. This is no place for you to stay.'

Higgledy-piggledy house was very sad. No one seemed to want a higgledy-piggledy house at all. Perhaps he should go back to the lonely sea-shore after all.

'Now, now,' clucked a kindly old hen, 'go down there – to the town. That's the place for a house like you.'

Higgledy-piggledy house was over-joyed. He raced away down the road towards the town, even though his blisters hurt. He went past the police station so fast it was lucky the policemen were having their supper, otherwise the higgledy-piggledy house might have been arrested for speeding. Past the post office and the supermarket, round the corner and then . . .

'Why, this is the place, the very place for me!' cried the higgledy-piggledy house. There, in a row, were higgledy-piggledy houses, all with their windows sloping this way and their doors sloping that, their ceilings all sagging and their floors that weren't flat.

There was a gap at one end of the row, just big enough for the higgledy-piggledy house to squeeze into. He pulled himself up as straight and tall as he could and there he stood.

Hardly anyone noticed the next day when the swirly-curly fog had gone that there was one more higgledy-piggledy house than there used to be. Except a higgledy-piggledy man who saw it and said,

'Why, that's just the house, the very house for me and my higgledy-piggledy family.'

So they all moved in. Sometimes the grey sea-gull came to rest on the higgledy-piggledy house's chimneys when he was flying that way.

And they all lived happily ever after.

Snow on the Mountain

Once upon a long time ago, Meralina Witchery was the best witch in Topshire. But, as the years went by, fewer and fewer people believed in magic and then hardly anyone wanted her magic spells. So Meralina became poorer and poorer until she couldn't even afford to feed Sammy, her black cat, any longer.

'Sammy,' she said, one grey October morning, 'we'll each have to go off into the world to make our own living. You're a good mouser and someone is sure to take you in and look after you.'

'What will you do?' mewed Sammy. He loved the witch and was very unhappy to think they had to part.

'Oh, I'll give up being a witch,' she sighed and she threw all her magic books into the stream which ran along underneath the window. 'I'll think of something. There must be lots of other things I could do.'

So, next day, in the cold light of early morning, Meralina and Sammy said goodbye to each other and set out alone.

Soon Meralina came to a town and found herself a job as a cook. But, she had only ever mixed magic spells before and she didn't know anything about ordinary cooking, so that at the end of the week, the lady of the house said,

'I'm afraid you'll have to go. Your cooking is terrible. It's given all of us indigestion.'

'Yes, I know,' agreed Meralina sadly. She too was beginning to feel unwell, after eating her own cooking for a week.

So off she went the next day to find some other kind of work.

This time, Meralina thought perhaps she could be a general help, by doing the house-cleaning for someone. But she had never done any real housework before, because her magic broom had done it all for her. So that at the end of the second week, the lady of the house said to her,

'I'm very much afraid you'll have to go. The house is dirtier than when you came.'

'Yes, I know,' agreed Meralina, looking miserably at the mess all around her. She gathered up her few belongings and set off the next day.

As she wandered down the road, a notice in a shop window caught her eye,

'Cat-lover wanted,' it said. 'Kind person to help in Cats' Home.'

Meralina cheered up at once.

'That's just the job for me,' she exclaimed.

Meralina worked hard at the Cats' Home because she was so happy to be with all those cats and they loved her too. She hardly noticed that the helpings of food were rather small and she didn't really mind. But, at the end of the week, Mr Porter, the owner of the Cats' Home said to her,

'I'm truly sorry Meralina, but I'm afraid you'll have to go.'

'Why?' cried Meralina, 'I've worked so hard and I really have tried to do things right.'

'Yes, I know you have,' replied **Mr** Porter kindly. 'But you see, I have only just enough money to pay your wages for one week. As it is, I hardly have any money to buy food for the cats.'

'Then I'll work for nothing,' answered Meralina, 'if only you will let me stay.'

Mr Porter shook his head.

'No Meralina. I couldn't let you do that. You must take the money you've **earned** and you'll soon find yourself another job.'

So with tears in her eyes, Meralina set off for the next town. But she always tried not to be unhappy for long, so she soon dried her tears and said to herself,

'I know what I'll do. With the money I've earned so far, I'll buy myself a cat. It won't be the same as Sammy, but it will cheer me up a bit.'

She walked down the High Street, straight into the first pet shop she came to and asked for a black cat. The shopkeeper looked quite startled.

'You must be a stranger,' he replied. 'Don't you know there aren't any cats here?'

'Why not?'

'Because,' said the shopkeeper, dropping his voice to a whisper, 'they've all been frightened away by white mice.'

'WHAT!' Meralina could hardly believe her ears.

'It's true,' went on the shopkeeper, drawing her over to the window. 'You see that mountain . . .'

'The one with the snow on top?'

'That's not snow! Those are white mice. Thousands of them. And when it gets dark, they come creeping down into the town and eat up everything they can find.'

'Well I'll soon put a stop to that!'

Meralina had forgotten for the moment that she was no longer a witch and she rushed off towards the zig-zag path which led to the foot of the mountain.

'There's a huge reward for anyone who can,' the shopkeeper called after her.

But when Meralina arrived at the foot of the mountain and chanted her magic spell, three times forwards, one time backwards and seven times back-to-front – nothing happened! Nothing at all. The mountain still looked exactly the same.

'Oh dear,' sobbed Meralina, 'I'm no good at anything at all. I can't do anything right.'

She wandered along without really noticing where she was going until she found herself back at the Cats' Home. Mr Porter was so pleased to see her again, but Meralina noticed that he and all the cats had been crying and they were thinner than ever.

'They're so hungry,' he explained, 'I had nothing to give them for breakfast. There's just one morsel of smelly cheese between the lot of them for their dinner and they're not very keen on that.'

'Never mind,' exclaimed Meralina, who had just had a great idea. 'Quickly, rub each cat's paws with the cheese and tell them to follow me.'

Off went Meralina and all the cats trotted behind her to the town by the mountain. And, in the darkness of the night, when the white mice, lured by the strong cheesy smell came creeping and squeaking down the mountainside . . . each one . . . walked . . . straight . . . into the waiting mouth of a VERY hungry cat.

When the sun rose over the purple mountain the next morning, the people looked up and saw the mountain no longer had its topping of white. How they cheered and what great celebrations they had! Meralina was given a big reward. Her name was in all the newspapers and she even appeared on television. She became so rich and famous that Sammy was soon able to find her again at Mr Porter's Cats' Home. And, just as in all the old-fashioned fairy stories, Meralina, Mr Porter, Sammy and all the other cats, lived happily ever after.

The Runaway Piano

There were so many things in Mr Dick's Junk Shop that he had quite forgotten what some of them were. There were tables with funny legs, chairs with wobbly backs, beds with broken springs and all kinds of other useless bric-a-brac.

'What a muddle!' Mrs Dick would grumble. 'Why don't you get rid of some of it?'

'Yes, yes, all right my dear, I will,' Mr Dick would murmur. But he never did.

Right over in a dark and dusty corner, hidden away by piles of furniture, was an old piano. It had once belonged to a famous pianist, but that was a very long time ago. It had once had right across its front, in gleaming golden lettering, its name – TRUMPELMETZEL. But over the years, the lettering had faded away until only the word 'TRUMPEL' remained.

There was no one to play Trumpel now, only Grey Whisker Mouse who ran over the keys at night-time.

There was no one to listen to Trumpel's music either, except that is for Jumbo, the white wooden elephant with only one tusk, standing close beside the piano in the dark corner. He loved to hear the sounds that Trumpel made when Grey Whisker Mouse ran over the keys.

'What wonderful music,' he would say. 'Please, Trumpel, let us have that tune again.'

One day when Mrs Dick came down into the shop she complained again.

'It's about time you turned out most of this rubbish. That piano, for instance, that should be chopped up for firewood *and* that dreadful old white elephant – just look at it – it's only got one tusk!'

'I suppose you're right my dear,' sighed Mr Dick. 'Nobody seems to want such things nowadays. I'll see about it tomorrow.'

That night, when the pale moonbeams shone through the darkness into Mr Dick's shop, Grey Whisker Mouse came out to scamper over the piano's ivory keys. He couldn't understand why the piano played such a sad tune.

'What's wrong, Trumpel?' he asked.

'Didn't you hear what Mr Dick said?' wailed Trumpel. 'Tomorrow I shall be chopped up for firewood.'

'Why don't you run away?' asked Grey Whisker Mouse.

'How can I?' cried the piano, 'I may have legs but *I* can't move them.'

'If only I could help,' boomed Jumbo. 'Real elephants are very strong. If only I could move.'

'I could help you,' said Grey Whisker Mouse, 'I'll get all my family. Together we could all push. We could move you.'

'Thank you,' replied Trumpel sadly, 'I'm afraid I would be much too heavy for little mice like you to move.'

'But there are lots of us. Just you wait and see,' answered Grey Whisker Mouse, eagerly. He gave a low whistle and out of every nook and cranny, up from the floorboards, down from the rafters came Grey Whisker's brothers, sisters, Aunts, Uncles and cousins in their hundreds. Together they pushed and pulled and panted – but they could not manage to move the piano even an inch.

'Oh dear! What shall we do now?' cried all the mice.

'If only I could move,' boomed Jumbo again.

A blue moon had risen high in the sky and was shining full on the white elephant. And, in the magic moonlight, something wonderful happened.

'Look! Look at Jumbo! He moved! I'm sure he moved!' squeaked Grey Whisker Mouse excitedly.

'Yes,' boomed Jumbo. 'At last! I really can help now. But I'll have to act fast. This kind of magic only happens once in a blue moon and it doesn't last long.'

He was *so* eager to help and, before any of the mice could stop him, he pushed against the piano with all his strength. The piano started to move. It slid right across the floor, slowly at first, then faster and faster until with a crash it had burst the shop door right open.

'Oh no,' groaned Grey Whisker Mouse. 'Now you've done it. You'll have woken everybody up. Both of you, escape quickly while you can.'

'Yes, I think perhaps we'd better,' said the elephant slowly and he tried to lower his head to push the piano again . . . But nothing happened. The moon had disappeared behind a cloud.

'Oh dear,' groaned the elephant, 'I said this magic wouldn't last. I can't move at all now.'

Jumbo was so sad he would have cried but his wooden eyelids would not even blink.

Fortunately Trumpel had landed out in the street on all four legs and was not hurt at all, only rather shaken.

Lights were being switched on in all the shops and houses round about. People came running. A policeman was called and even Mr Dick woke up and came downstairs to see what had happened.

'How did that piano get there,' puzzled Mr Dick, rubbing the sleep out of his eyes.

'Burglars, I expect sir,' replied the policeman, who thought he knew all about such things. 'You must have some very valuable things in your shop.'

'Well, I don't know about that,' said Mr Dick truthfully, still wondering how the piano, which six strong men were now carrying back into the shop, had got into the street.

'Yes. He has,' Mrs Dick was saying firmly. She had just come down in a red dressing gown with her hair all in curlers. 'He has lots of priceless antiques. *Very* valuable.'

There was a buzz of excitement through the crowd and a newspaper reporter in the front row wrote busily in his notebook.

The next morning, there was quite a queue of customers when Mr Dick went down to open his shop. They had seen in the morning's newspapers the report of the attempted burglary and, as soon as they read that all the old things in Mr Dick's Junk Shop were priceless antiques, they wanted to be the first to buy them. People were buying things so quickly, there soon would not be any need for Mr Dick to turn out, or chop up, anything. Although no one seemed to want the old piano or the white elephant with only one tusk.

Mr Dick was just about to close the shop so that he and Mrs Dick could have their dinner when there was a great banging at the shop door.

'Whoever can that be?' said Mr Dick crossly, then, 'Oh it's you. Come in young man.'

He recognized the young man on the doorstep. He was a music student who lived down the street in a poky little room over a Chinese restaurant.

'The piano,' panted the young man, who had been running hard, 'I heard you have a piano for sale. Can I see it?'

'Mr Dick will let you have it cheap,' said Mrs Dick, before her husband could say anything, 'if you buy that little wooden elephant as well.'

The young man hesitated. He had not really thought about buying a white elephant – he could hardly afford to buy a piano as it was. Then he ran his fingers gently over Trumpel's keys – giving Grey Whisker Mouse who was still inside the piano, quite a fright.

'I like the sound it makes,' smiled the young man. He looked at the white elephant. It seemed to be smiling too.

'All right,' said the young man. 'Somehow I think that elephant belongs with the piano, so I will take them both.'

Jumbo was so happy and so was Trumpel!

'You won't regret it, young man,' Mr Dick was saying. 'Why with a beautiful piano like that you'll be a famous musician one day, I shouldn't wonder.'

And do you know, he was right! But that's another story.

Horatio Newt

Horatio Newt was born one sunny spring morning upon a water-lily leaf. He was a funny little creature, inside a shell so clear and thin you could see right inside, all curled up with his nose against his tail. Sometimes, inside his shell, he would wriggle and twist, as if to make himself more comfortable, and he would sing:

'I'm a growing little newt,
I'm a stretching little newt,
I'm a cute little newt – I am.'

Until one day, when he was doing this . . . crick-crack-crang . . . the egg-shell broke and out slipped Horatio into the water, down to the bottom of the pond, where he lay very still among the water-weeds for a while.

'Arrh! I am glad that's over! All that growing and stretching and everything.'

But still Horatio went on growing, even when he was out of the shell. Tiny legs began to form and soon he found he could dart and dash about the pond faster than ever. Horatio became bigger, stronger and more handsome until he was like a tiny dragon with a crest of gold upon his head. Then he would climb up the muddy bank and rest upon a flat stone at the shallow end of the pond, looking at himself in the water and singing:

'I'm a handsome newt,
I'm a brave big newt,
I'm a fabulous newt – that's me.'

Mrs Newt, who wasn't quite so beautiful to look at, was afraid to come out of the water. Only at night-time would she creep out in search of food. But she was worried about Horatio.

'Oh Horatio . . . oh!' she would wail. 'Come back this minute. You know it's safer down here than on land. Horatio . . . oh!'

'Oh fiddle-de-dee. Not me. I'm as safe as . . . Ooooh goodness me!'

Mrs Newt never heard what Horatio was as safe as, because just at that moment he was picked up by a great big land-monster and put into a glass jar.

Big eyes stared at Horatio through the jar. Other land-monsters came to look at him. What would they do to him? Were they going to eat him, gobble him up in one gulp? Horatio felt very frightened.

Then one of the land-monsters spoke,
     'Look Miss, isn't he lovely?'
     'Yes he certainly is. Let's take him
back to school for our aquarium, shall we
children?'
     'Oh yes, let's, please Miss.'
     Poor Horatio! And in a troubled, trembly voice he sang:

> 'Oh mercy me!
> I'm a worried little newt,
> A scared little newt – that's me!'

But he needn't have worried. He was
soon in the school classroom where he
was tipped out into the aquarium. He
swam around, taking a good look at the
strange new place. It was cold and light,
not a bit like the pond. 'What funny sort
of water this is! *And* it's got hard edges.
Ouch!'

His nose had come up against the glass
side and he wondered why he couldn't get
through it. But there were snails and
water-weed in the aquarium like there
were in his own pond, so, he didn't feel
quite so strange after a while, and the
land-monsters brought him scraps of raw
meat, which he gobbled up in no time.
Even so Horatio was miserable. He missed the pond very much and he wanted
more than anything else to find his way
back there somehow.
     Then he noticed that the land-monsters
went away every afternoon at the same
time and didn't come back until the next
morning. So every night, he crawled up
the sides of the aquarium and, then one
night, he discovered that someone had
forgotten to put the cover on the
aquarium.

63

So, Horatio slithered out of the tank and down on to the dusty classroom floor. Over the floor, across the classroom, down the corridor, out through a crack under the door and through the playground he crawled. Then away down the hill towards the pond with the two wooden bridges. Now, in land-monster strides the distance between the aquarium and the pond takes no time at all, but for a tiny newt like Horatio, it was a long and difficult journey through an unknown land.

'But I'm a strong little newt,
    A brave little newt,
A never-give-up little newt – that's me.'

And he didn't give up. On and on he crawled until at last he reached the pond again. Wearily he slipped into the water. At once a crowd of newts came swimming towards him. He tried to call out to them, but he was too weak and tired.

The other newts crowded round him and they didn't look at all friendly,

'Who are you?'

Horatio gulped and gasped and tried to tell them.

'He doesn't answer.'

'He's a stranger. He's an enemy.'

'Let's get rid of him. Attack and destroy!'

Angrily they swam towards him, tails lashing and jaws snapping, all ready to gobble him up. But as they came closer still, one cried out,

'Stop, oh stop. Can't you see, it's Horatio? Tell them it's you, Horatio,' pleaded Mrs Newt, swimming up close beside him. And he gasped:

'I'm a sad little newt,
    I'm a tired little newt,
But I'm a glad-to-be-home newt!
    – that's me.'

'No, no it can't be! Is it possible?' cried all the newts.

'Yes, of course it is. Don't you think *I* know my own Horatio?' demanded Mrs Newt.

It was certainly hard for them to believe that this miserable creature before them was the once handsome Horatio. But then, they knew nothing of Horatio's adventures until, when he grew stronger, Horatio told them all about the land-monsters. That's probably why when the schoolchildren come down now each spring, looking for newts for their aquarium, they never seem to find any. None of them wants to be caught like Horatio was.

Father Christmas and the Mickets

Early one Christmas Eve, Father Christmas was about to set off in his sleigh when he suddenly remembered something. Out he hopped and ran back into his workshop.

'It wouldn't do to forget the Mickets,' he said, heaving another sack into his sleigh. 'Oh no I mustn't forget *them*.'

'Who are the Mickets?' asked the youngest of Father Christmas's reindeer.

'Why don't you know? No, of course, you're new. You haven't been on one of my Christmas journeys before have you? Well, off we go, little fellow and you'll soon find out.'

Through the starry night they went. Over fields, houses and trees, so far away below, they looked like toy farms and toy towns.

Father Christmas was feeling very happy. He was thinking of all the children fast asleep in their beds and what a joyful day Christmas Day would be for everyone. He began to sing, 'Jingle bells, jingle bells, jingle . . . Goodness gracious me! What was *that*?'

Something like an enormous silver pencil swished through the darkness above him. He looked at it through his long-range spectacles.

'Why I do believe it's a spaceship!'

It was indeed. A spaceman from Earth was on his way to the Moon.

Father Christmas had so many presents to deliver that Christmas Eve, he soon forgot about the spaceman. Only one sack remained, when at last he climbed back into his sleigh.

'Now for the Mickets,' he called to his reindeer. He winked at the youngest one.

Up again into the sky they soared. Up, up and away, up towards the Moon and then on to the Moon, where they landed as gently as a feather.

'Urr-choo! Arr-choo!' sneezed Father Christmas, shaking the moondust from his whiskers.

'Bless you!' said a voice behind him and Father Christmas spun round in surprise. There, on the Moon, was the spaceman from Earth. The spaceman was even more surprised to see Father Christmas.

'Father Christmas! I didn't expect to find you and your reindeer on the Moon!' he said.

'What did you expect to find?' asked Father Christmas.

'I came to find out if there are any living creatures on the Moon. Everyone on Earth is waiting for my message.'

'Well, well, well,' laughed Father Christmas, 'you can take it from me there aren't any living creatures at all *on* the Moon.'

Then, because the spaceman looked disappointed, Father Christmas said, 'But you can say you met *me* and you can wish everyone on Earth a Merry Christmas from me.'

The spaceman cheered up at once and started off for home immediately. When he looked round again to wave goodbye, Father Christmas had vanished, because the moment the spaceman turned his back, Father Christmas sank lower and lower into the moondust, down into a secret Moon tunnel until he was right inside a huge cave, beautiful and shiny, like the inside of a sea-shell. This is where the Mickets lived, right inside the Moon.

The clever Mickets had once lived on Earth. Long, long ago they had built themselves a spaceship and set off for the Moon. The spaceship was made from magic stones from the gigantic stones on Micket Hill. (Some of them are still there today – wise people from all over the world come to look at them and wonder about them.)

Now, when the Mickets' stone spaceship landed on the Moon, because it was so heavy, it crashed right through the surface and broke into billions of pieces. And that's why there's so much moondust! Luckily, the Mickets were not hurt in the crash-landing.

When the Mickets explored the moon caves, they found rivers of sweet cool water and delicious fruit, like silver grapes, and they didn't want to return to Micket Hill where cruel wars were being fought. They wanted to stay in the peaceful moon caves for ever.

Christmas Eve is the one night of the year when all Mickets stay up late to talk and sing to Father Christmas. So, as soon as they saw him, they crowded round him asking, 'What kept you so long?'

Father Christmas told them about the spaceman from Earth.

'Ooooh dear! You didn't tell him about us, did you?'

'Of course not! He was only looking for life *on* the moon. I shall never tell anyone that you live inside the Moon. So cheer up. Come and get your presents and sing to me.'

So they sang to him, a prayer for peace and joy to all mankind.

The spaceman heard the Mickets' song as he travelled back to Earth and wondered what the strange and beautiful music was and where it came from. None of the clever scientists back on Earth could explain it. But we know, don't we? And, if Father Christmas can keep a secret, so can we.

Tickletoes and the Slippers

Tickletoes was a naughty little creature as small as a shoehorn and as quiet as a mouse. He lived in a dark and dusty corner on a shelf in Mr Martin's shoe shop. Mr Martin didn't even know he was there, for Tickletoes was very careful to hide away

Sometimes at night-time when Mr Martin was fast asleep and Tickletoes was feeling good, he would creep out and tidy up all the piles of shoes which customers had tried on during the day. But sometimes when Tickletoes was feeling naughty, he would play all kinds of tricks, like tangling up the shoe-laces and putting shoes into the wrong boxes. Then poor Mr Martin would scratch his head and say to his customers.

'Dear, dear! I just don't know how it is that things get into such a muddle.'

One dull grey winter's morning, Tickletoes was feeling very naughty indeed. From his secret pocket he took a little box of red-hot-tickly-toe-powder and sprinkled it into all the pairs of slippers upon the shelf. Now whoever tried the slippers on would have feet as hot as red-hot pokers until the slippers were taken off.

'Giggledy, piggledy, hoppity-he,
Now some fun there'll surely be!'

chuckled Tickletoes.

No sooner had he said this than the shop-bell rang and in came pretty Miss Smart. Tickletoes crept to the edge of the shelf and listened hoping that she had come to buy a pair of slippers.

But Miss Smart hadn't come for slippers.

'I would like a pair of silver dancing shoes, please Mr Martin,' she said.

'Certainly my dear,' replied Mr Martin and he found her a spinkly-sparkly pair which suited her pretty feet exactly.

'Bother,' muttered Tickletoes crossly. 'Why couldn't she buy slippers instead!'

The next customer that morning was Mr Bell, with his little girl Ann. Tickletoes ran to the edge of the shelf again and listened. But they hadn't come to buy slippers either.

'We would like some new snow-boots for Ann,' said Mr Bell.

'Certainly. I think I have just the very thing,' replied Mr Martin, taking out a **red pair** from one of the lower shelves.

The snow-boots fitted Ann perfectly, so she and Mr Bell went off feeling very pleased. But Tickletoes was growing crosser and crosser.

Presently an old lady came hobbling into the shop.

'Can you find me your very largest pair of warm slippers please,' she asked Mr Martin.

'Just take a seat, madam, whilst I have a look on the shelf where the large sizes are kept,' called Mr Martin, climbing up the little metal ladder he used to reach the topmost shelves.

'Tee-hee,' giggled Tickletoes to himself, spinning round and round with excitement. 'The old woman will have toes like toasted kippers, when she puts on a pair of these slippers.'

'Dear me,' exclaimed Mr Martin, reaching out to take a pair of brown leather slippers from the shelf. 'How dusty they all are.'

He took a deep breath and blew quite a cloud of Tickletoes' red-hot-tickly-toe-powder off the slippers. Tickletoes who was taken by surprise was blown over backwards and rolled over and over into the far corner of the shelf.

'There,' said Mr Martin briskly, climbing down the ladder and putting the slippers on the stool beside the old lady, 'would you like to try them on?'

'No thank you,' laughed the old lady. 'They're not for me. But they look just the right size for my husband. Put them into a parcel right away please, because I have to hurry to catch the bus back home.'

Up on the slipper shelf, Tickletoes was very uncomfortable. The cloud of red-hot-tickly-toe-powder had covered him completely and he was so hot and tickly all over he just couldn't keep still. But that wasn't all. As soon as the old lady had gone, Mr Martin went to his broom cupboard, took out a feather duster and flicked it hard all over the slipper shelf, which made Tickletoes more tickly than ever.

You won't be surprised to hear that it was quite a long time before Tickletoes felt like being naughty again, after that.

And what happened to the slippers which the old lady bought? Well, she gave them to her husband that night, and although Mr Martin had blown off most of the powder there were just one or two grains left inside the lining. Just about enough to keep the old man's tired old toes warm and comfortable whenever he wore them. So that on cold winter days he would kiss the old woman and say happily,

'Thank you my dear for these beautiful slippers. They really are the cosiest pair I have ever had.'

Tom Tiddler

Round about and in and out of the tall reeds in the pond with the two wooden bridges, swam Tom Tiddler.

'That little tiddler's never still,' grumbled Grandpa Minnow to Grandma Minnow.

'He'll come to a bad end and that's for sure,' sighed the three Aunt Minnows to one another. But Tom Tiddler didn't hear them, or if he did, he took no notice.

He darted into an empty ice-cream carton which was floating in the water and he began to sing:

'We all live in a purple submarine . . . No! That's not right! It was either red or green . . .'

'Quiet Tom,' warned Mrs Tiddler. 'If the ducks hear you they'll come and gobble you up in no time at all.'

'I'm not scared of ducks!' said Tom, dashing in and out of the thick weeds at the bottom of the pond. He was pretending to be a secret agent, escaping from the duck enemy. His forty-three little brothers and sisters swam happily after him.

'Come on,' he shouted. 'Let's be rockets going up into space. Five, four, three, two, one . . . BLAST OFF!'

He zoomed up to the top of the water. There were ripples on the water, like tiny waves on a big sea, which meant . . .

'DANGER!' cried a tiny tiddler. 'There are ducks about! Dive for cover everyone.'

'I don't see any ducks,' said Tom. He pushed a floating leaf aside with his nose, so that he could see better. 'All I can see is a long stick with some funny pink stuff at the end of it and I'm going to find out what it is.'

'DANGER! DANGER! Dive for cover,' cried all the forty-three tiny tiddlers.

They shot down like silver arrows through the water to the stones and the thick weeds at the bottom of the pond.

'Got him!' shouted a boy's voice and Tom, who had swum right up against the pink stuff, felt himself lifted up in the air. He had been caught in the boy's pink fishing net.

'Let me see, Peter,' called a boy's voice.

He waded across to his friend and peered into the net at the squirming Tom Tiddler. 'Is that all? He's not very big, is he?'

'Well, at least I've caught one, which is more than you did,' said Peter. 'And if I take him home and feed him with worms, I expect he'll grow bigger.'

He shook Tom out of the net into a glass jar, which had a piece of string tied round it for a handle.

Tom swam round and round inside the jam jar, wondering if he could find a way out, but he only bumped his nose against the glass, so he stayed quite still and just wondered what would happen to him.

Suddenly there was a great rushing of feet and shouting of voices. A crowd of boys came through the trees, down the hill towards the pond.

'Quick!' called Peter. 'It's the "O" Gang. They look as if they're going to start a fight.'

Then the jam jar was hurriedly dumped down upon the ground.

'I'll take that!' said a boy with black boots, reaching out his hand for the jar.

'You won't!' said Peter. 'It's mine.'

The water in the jar slapped backward and forwards against the sides and Tom felt like a tiny boat in a great storm.

Then, 'Hey you lot, dive for cover,' shouted one of the other boys. 'It's the park-keeper.'

Most of the 'O' Gang dashed off towards a gap in the hedge.

The boy with black boots stopped to grab again at the jar. Peter struggled to get it away from him.

'Oh no you don't,' Peter said. 'He doesn't really belong to either of us.'

'But *I* want him,' argued the boy.

'No!' said Peter. He jerked the jar away from the boy with black boots and tipped Tom Tiddler back into the pond again . . .

Oh how wonderful it felt! Tom wriggled his tail happily and swam round and round in dizzy circles.

'Your mother's been looking for you and she's very cross because you didn't come when she called,' said Grandpa and Grandma Minnow.

'*We* thought the ducks had got you,' chorused the three Aunt Minnows.

'Something much worse than ducks tried to get me, but I got away,' boasted Tom Tiddler.

He flicked his silver-green tail and glided smoothly through the water, pretending he was a heroic battleship returning from a war.

'What was it?' asked the little minnows excitedly, crowding all around him. 'Tell us what it was.'

'*Something,*' replied Tom, with a shudder, 'very huge and horrible. *Boys,* I think they're called. Much, much worse than ducks. So mind *you* all beware of boys in future!'

The Magic Cloak

Once there was a poor young tailor with a handsome golden beard and gentle blue eyes. He loved his work and he worked very hard at making fine clothes. He lived all alone in a cold grey room behind his shop. Well, not quite alone, because every night a thin brown mouse called Clarence came to keep the tailor company and to share his supper with him.

The tailor took a lot of trouble over his work which meant his customers had to wait a long time for their new clothes and sometimes they would grumble.

'We can't wait any longer. We're going off to the shops where we can buy machine-made clothes right away.'

So, of course, the poor tailor grew even poorer. He could no longer pay his electricity bills. His electricity was cut off

and he could only work in the daylight or by dim candle-light after dark. Sometimes he could not even buy himself and Clarence enough food to eat.

One day, he was just going to the baker's shop to spend his last few pence when he noticed a picture in a carved wooden frame in Mr Dick's Junk shop window. It was a painting of rosy apples and golden oranges piled upon a table. Behind them stood a crusty loaf and a jug, and behind that, a rich draping – a cloth of wonderful glowing colours. It was the draping that caught the tailor's eye. He looked at the picture for a long time.

'Ah,' he sighed, 'there's a kind of magic in such beautiful things!'

'That's just what I always say,' said a voice behind him. It was Mr Dick, the Junk Shop owner, coming to the doorway of his shop. 'Why not buy it then?'

'I could only give you a few pence for it,' laughed the tailor.

'All right,' agreed Mr Dick, who was very kindhearted. He had hoped to sell the picture for a great deal more, but he could see the tailor was really taken with it.

The tailor went home and was so busy at his work and so pleased with his new painting all that day, he had no time to think about how hungry he was. That night when it grew too dark for him to work any more, he hammered a nail into the wall to hang up the picture.

Clarence came scuttering out of his mouse hole. He sat twitching his whiskers for a while. Then he squeaked to remind the tailor that he was there.

'Oh poor Clarence!' said the tailor sadly when he turned round and saw the little mouse, 'I haven't even a crumb for you.'

'Ah,' he said, running his fingers over the canvas as he hung the picture on the wall, 'I only wish the things in this picture were real.'

The picture grew suddenly heavy and, instead of feeling the flat canvas under his fingertips, he felt something round and lumpy. The tailor staggered to the table to rest his heavy burden. And then he saw that the wooden frame was now a wooden tray and on it, *real* fruit, a *real* crusty loaf and a *real* jug-full of creamy milk. But, that wasn't all, the rich draping of material at the back of the picture had become a *real* roll of cloth which trailed across the floor in the darkness like a shower of moonbeams.

'Oh,' exclaimed the tailor, hardly able to believe his eyes. 'How beautiful! It's pure magic! With cloth like this, I could make a cloak fit for a princess.'

He picked up one of the apples which had rolled off the table and took a bite. It was sweet and juicy. Then he took up the loaf and broke it into pieces.

'Come along, Clarence,' he called, 'we've a feast to share tonight!'

When they had both eaten their fill, the tailor took the last candle from his store-cupboard and lit it. He laid the moonbeam-coloured cloth upon the table and took up his scissors. He stitched away until, in the early morning light, the cloak was quite finished.

'Fit for a princess,' said the tailor, as he draped the cloak in his window for everyone to see.

He was just about to fall asleep, after working so hard, when there was a great hammering at the door. When the tailor opened the door, there, on the doorstep stood a young lady as beautiful as a princess.

'I would like to buy the cloak in the window to wear to the Mayor's Ball tonight,' she said, thinking what a sleepy young man the tailor was, as he stood there yawning and trying not to fall asleep.

'I will pay you whatever you ask,' she told him.

'Please try it on,' suggested the tailor. He put the cloak around her shoulders and she looked more beautiful than ever.

That evening at the Mayor's Ball, everyone was dazzled by the beauty of the young lady in her moonbeam-coloured cloak and they all wanted to know who had made such a wonderful garment.

It wasn't long before the tailor had hundreds of customers who didn't mind waiting for the perfect clothes he made. He has become quite rich now and he has a wife to share his life. She is as beautiful as a princess. And Clarence? The tailor and his wife still share their supper with him. Only now Clarence is no longer a thin little mouse. He's a very fat little mouse, because he never goes hungry any more.

Plum Jam for Tea

In a garden, on a tree, grew ten beautiful plums. Down in a hole in the ground beside that tree, all by himself, lived Stinger Wasp. He lived by himself because no one liked him. Even the other wasps were frightened of him and his sharp stinging tail. Stinger Wasp didn't care. He was waiting for the plums on the tree to ripen. He just loved sweet, juicy, golden plums.

Now, those plums belonged to a greedy old man. Every morning after breakfast he counted the plums to make sure they were all still there.

Whenever the old man's wife pegged washing on the clothes-line, he called out, 'Be careful, old lady!'

Whenever birds fluttered around the plum tree, the old man rushed out shouting, 'Shoo! Go away!'

Whenever the lady-next-door and her little boy looked over the fence, the old man glared at them, as if to say, 'Don't you dare touch my plums!'

Now, one night there was a terrible storm. And those ten plums were blown right off the tree. So when Stinger Wasp came out of his hole the next morning, there they were on the ground. He buzzed round and round with delight. Then he burrowed right into the biggest one, eating as he went, until only the fine point of his stinging tail was sticking out.

That was why he didn't see the old man and the old lady when they came out into the garden. *That* was why he didn't know that the old lady was gathering up the plums in a bowl and taking them into the kitchen. The old lady put the plums in the sink to wash them. She turned on the cold water. Then she went to make the old man's dinner.

Stinger Wasp didn't like cold water. He pulled himself out of the plum, buzzing angrily. He shook the water off his wings and few up to the top of the kitchen window where it was sunny and dry. And there he stayed.

When the old lady had washed up after dinner, the old man said, 'Now you can make those plums into jam for my tea.'

When the plum jam was ready, the old lady poured it into a pot and put a cover over. Then she left it on the kitchen table to cool.

'Old lady,' called the old man, 'let's have tea in the garden.'

The old lady carried all the tea-things on a tray into the garden. Soon she called. 'Tea's ready!'

The old man came into the garden, and so did Stinger Wasp. They were both looking forward to plum jam for tea. The old man sat down, put the biggest piece of bread and butter on his plate and took the lid off the jam pot. This was the moment Stinger Wasp had been waiting for. He flew straight towards the jam.

'Go away! Shoo!' said the old man. But Stinger Wasp didn't go away. Every time the old man reached out for the jam, Stinger Wasp made a dive for it too. The old man jumped up and waved his arms around. This made Stinger Wasp angry. He danced up and down in a fury. Then the old man tried to chase Stinger Wasp away, but soon Stinger Wasp was chasing *him*. Up the path, ran the old man. he rushed indoors and closed the door and all the windows.

After a little while the old lady called, 'Aren't you coming back to have your tea?'

The old man was certain he could still hear Stinger Wasp buzzing outside the window, so he called back, 'No. I'm not. I don't want any tea today.'

The old lady was about to pour herself a cup of tea, when she saw the lady-next-door and her little boy looking over the fence. She smiled at them and said, 'Would you like to come round? There's plum jam for tea.'

They both said, 'Yes please.'

So the old lady, the lady-next-door and her little boy all had plum jam for tea. But, neither the greedy old man nor Stinger Wasp had plum jam for *their* tea that day.

When the Sun Shone and Shone

Early one spring morning the Sun leapt out of bed. He pushed away the clouds and said, 'Today, I will shine and shine all day.'

And so he did.

The birds began to sing in the sunshine. Green shoots began to grow. Spiders came out to spin new webs. The water in the lakes and ponds sparkled and shone too. Everyone smiled and said, 'How lovely to see the sunshine!'

For it had been a long cold winter.

The Sun looked at his reflection in the water. He smiled too. 'It's good to know,' he said, 'that everyone loves me.'

At the end of the day, the Sun did not want to go to bed. 'Oh no,' he said, 'I want to stay in the sky all night through.'

'You can't!' cried the clouds. 'It wouldn't be right! It's the time for the Moon to come out at night. Besides, you must rest if you want to be at your best tomorrow.'

The Sun was feeling a bit sleepy. So he agreed, 'Oh well, all right. But I'll be up early and I'll shine again all day tomorrow.'

And so he did.

The birds all sang. The grass grew fresh and green. Spring flowers burst into bloom. The water in the lakes and ponds shone like polished gold.

Again everyone smiled and said, 'How lovely to see the sunshine!'

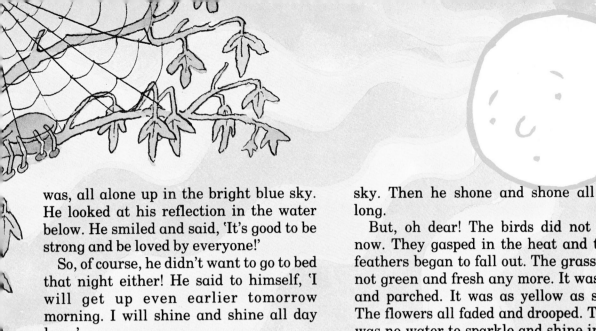

was, all alone up in the bright blue sky. He looked at his reflection in the water below. He smiled and said, 'It's good to be strong and be loved by everyone!'

So, of course, he didn't want to go to bed that night either! He said to himself, 'I will get up even earlier tomorrow morning. I will shine and shine all day long.'

And so he did.

So it went on, day after day, for a long, long time. Every day the Sun rose high and chased the clouds right out of the

The Sun was pleased. He pushed the clouds right away from him. There he

sky. Then he shone and shone all day long.

But, oh dear! The birds did not sing now. They gasped in the heat and their feathers began to fall out. The grass was not green and fresh any more. It was dry and parched. It was as yellow as sand. The flowers all faded and drooped. There was no water to sparkle and shine in the lakes and ponds. They had been dried right up by the Sun.

Everyone frowned and said, 'This Sun's too strong for anyone.'

The Sun looked for his reflection in the water. But it was nowhere to be seen. There was no water below, only dry parched earth.

This time the Sun did not smile. He was sad that no one was pleased to see him any more. He was also beginning to feel very tired. Although he still got up early, it wasn't quite so easy to rise up high in the sky.

'Oh dear,' he sighed, 'I thought it was good to be strong. But no one's glad to see me any more. What am I to do?'

From the earth a thin silver mist was rising through the air, cool and caressing, whispering, 'Rest now. The earth needs rain. Please let the clouds bring the rain.'

Soon, soft white clouds had gathered round the Sun. They were all around him. He was too tired to push them away. He sank down into them and slept whilst the raindrops fell – pitter, patter, splitter, splash!

Pitter, patter, the raindrops fell on to the parched earth, the leaves, and the flowers until they were fresh and bright again.

Pitter patter fell the raindrops on the spiders' webs until they shone like diamonds.

Pitter patter the raindrops fell and filled the lakes and ponds once more.

Everyone smiled to see the rain making everything fresh again and they said, 'Let's hope the Sun will shine again tomorrow.'

And so he did – but not quite so fiercely this time.

Hetty Hippo's Secret

Not every family has a pet like Hetty. She is very special. She has short thick legs, a horny grey skin and a stumpy tail. She belongs to the Smith family. They can't quite remember how she came.

'I think she got here on a No. 14 bus,' said Mrs Smith. 'Anyway, we're very glad to have her. Hetty is such a lovely hippopotamus. And really, she is just like one of us.'

Now all the Smith family loved her. Mrs Smith, Mr Smith, and of course, Jim and Tina. They spent lots of time playing together. Whenever you passed the Smiths' house, you could hear Hetty's great feet clumping – THUMP, THUMP, CLUMP, CLUMP, around the place, upstairs and down. So, without a doubt, you knew there was a hippo about.

Sometimes when Mr and Mrs Smith were quietly watching TV after the children were in bed in the evening, Hetty's feet could be heard through the sitting room ceiling – CLUMP, CLUMP, THUMP, THUMP.

Mr Smith would get quite cross and say, 'What a din those children are making! The whole house is shaking. Shouldn't they be asleep in bed?'

Mrs Smith would only smile and say, 'No, no dear. It's not the children. That's Hetty. Hippos need to play sometimes you know.'

But even Mrs Smith got a bit cross when a chunk of plaster fell off the ceiling into her late night cup of tea.

She said, 'I do think Hetty might be more careful where she puts her feet!'

Now, Hetty had a secret, which she hadn't told to anyone.

One day, she'd seen a programme on TV. It was all about ballet dancing. Hetty had said to herself, 'Oooh, that's what I want to be – a ballet-dancing hippo. If I practise hard enough, why, one day I might even be on TV.'

She hadn't told anyone in the Smith family because they might laugh at her. That was why Hetty practised her dancing when she thought no one was about.

Jim and Tina did not guess her secret. Neither did Mr Smith. But Mrs Smith guessed. It was one night after a rather large bit of plaster had fallen on her head, and Mr Smith had said, 'Something's got to be done about that clumsy hippo.'

Mrs Smith replied, 'Of course dear! It's all too clear! It's come to me at last! Hetty's trying to teach herself to dance. She must join a ballet class.'

Sure enough, two days later Mrs Smith took Hetty along to the nearest ballet class. Hetty was excited but feeling rather shy. She looked quite a picture in her dancing shoes and pink frilly frou-frou which kind Mrs Smith had made for her.

The dancing class teacher, Miss Grace Sotay, seemed somewhat surprised. She said to Mrs Smith, 'It is rather unusual for someone of Hetty's shape and size to want to be a ballet dancer.'

'Well,' said Mrs Smith sharply, 'you can at least let her try.'

Miss Grace agreed. She told Hetty to stand in the back row and be ready to dance as soon as the music started. When Miss Grace nodded her head, the pianist, Miss Herd, began to play.

At the sound of the music, Hetty got quite carried away. With eyes tight closed, she leapt up on her toes. She twirled and she whirled in the air. CLUMP, CLUMP, THUMP, THUMP

went Hetty's feet. Soon she was in the centre of the stage. All the other children in the dancing class ran out of her way. She had the stage to herself.

SHAKE, SHAKE, QUAKE, QUAKE, went the floor under Hetty's dancing feet.

'STOP!' cried Miss Grace. She was afraid the floor might break.

Hetty didn't hear her. She was listening only to the music. Miss Herd, the pianist, didn't hear her. She too had her eyes closed and she was rather deaf.

Again Miss Grace cried, 'STOP!'

But, too late. With a CLUMP, CLUMP, THUMP, SHAKE, QUAKE, CRASH – the floor did break.

Then everyone rushed to help Hetty up on her feet. Everyone, that is, except Miss Herd, who went on playing, quite unconcerned.

Mrs Smith was so glad to see that Hetty was not hurt at all. She told Miss Grace that Mr Smith would soon mend the hole in the floor.

'I do not think,' Miss Grace told her, somewhat icily, 'that your hippo, Hetty, will ever be suitable to dance in any ballet.'

Mrs Smith had to agree. But she was afraid Hetty might cry, so quickly she said,

'Never mind. We'll soon think of something else you can do.'

'Oh yes,' said Hetty, smiling most sweetly. She had been gazing spellbound at Miss Herd, who all the while, had been playing the piano, quite unconcerned.

'I've made up my mind,' thought Hetty, 'but I shan't say a word. It's the piano I'm now going to learn to play. Perhaps if I practise and practise, why one day, I might play on TV.'

But, she decided not to tell anyone, not just yet – that would be her secret.

The Monster and his Pet

Many hundreds of years ago, in the Deep Blue Lake, there lived a family of monsters. They were the ugliest things you ever saw but they were gentle shy creatures and hardly ever showed their faces above water, all except Young Monster.

He would swim up to the surface of the Lake and watch the boys playing on the shore. He thought what fun they must be having and often wished he could play with them. And that gave him an idea.

'*Why* can't I have one as a pet?' he wailed to his mother.

'Because,' explained his mother wearily, 'I've told you a hundred times already. *Boys* don't make good pets. They don't keep well in water and they're not very pretty.'

'Why not have a fish instead?' suggested his father. 'They're much nicer than boys.'

Young Monster, in a sulk, dived down to the bottom of the Lake, sending such a stream of bubbles up to the surface that the fishermen in their boats looked uneasily at one another, wondering if the stories of monsters in the Lake were really true after all.

'I'll ask Grandpa what he thinks,' said Young Monster.

But Grandpa was fast asleep in the mud and snoring mud bubbles.

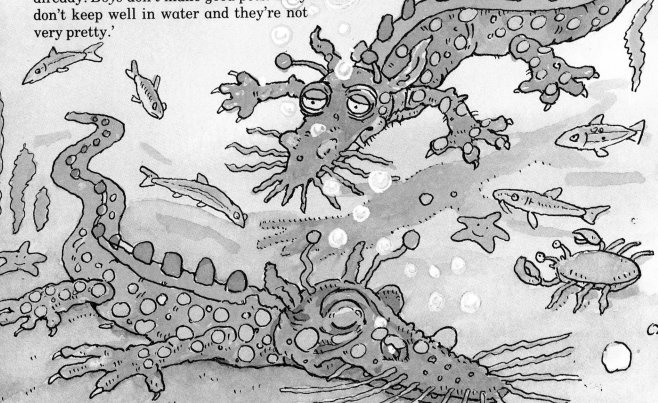

So, Young Monster swam to the top of the Lake again, climbed out of the water and went across the land in search of a boy.

It was summertime. The children of the vilage had been helping with the harvest in Sir Roger Whitesword's fields. For Sir Roger had been called away to fight a fierce battle in another part of the land.

Everyone was resting under the hedgerow in the shade, when the Monster picked up the nearest slumbering boy and ran off with him to the lakeside cave.

Now the boy was Sir Roger's only son James, and all the people loved him. Armed with sticks and staves, they followed the Monster's footprints down to the cave and were about to attack the Monster, when James came running out shouting,

'Don't hurt him! He's quite friendly and only wants to play.'

The people soon found the Monster meant no harm, but few were brave enough to come near him, because he was so ugly.

That summer, James taught the Monster to play cricket. He used his long horny tail as a bat and they had wonderful times together. But Sir Roger's army was being badly beaten and driven back towards the village.

'I must go and help my father to fight the Enemy,' James told the Monster.

'Let me help,' begged the Monster. 'Tell your people to come to this cave and . . . Oh yes, and tell them to bring a sack of flour and some hairbrushes with them.'

James was puzzled by this strange request but he did as he was told. All the people from the village came at once to the Monster's cave. So, as the Enemy advanced triumphantly, they found the village was deserted. Not one person was to be seen in the houses, shops, even in the school – not one single child.

'Something strange is going on here,' said the Enemy General and his army began to feel uneasy.

The Enemy had almost reach the cave when suddenly out ran all the villagers, screaming and shouting, white-faced and with their hair standing straight up on end. They looked as if they had all just seen something quite horrible. Of course the Enemy couldn't possibly know that the people's faces were only white with flour and that their hair had been carefully brushed that way!

Then, out of the cave, came Young Monster himself. He had practised all the morning making ugly faces at his reflection in the Lake. He looked a terrible sight as he glared and roared at the advancing army. They shook in their shoes *so* much that their rattling armour could be heard for miles. Then they took to their heels and ran off like the wind.

That night, there was great rejoicing in the village. Sir Roger gave a party and everyone was invited. A monster chair was found for Young Monster to sit in. It had been made long ago for a very fat ancestor of Sir Roger's. Young Monster felt very proud, sitting at the long table, with James beside him.

But, when some of the village people were full of good food and good wine, they began to boast of their cleverness in frightening the Enemy away. Then they began to plot.

'With iron chains,' said one, 'we could harness the Monster to a great chariot.'

'With great whips we could drive him on.'

'We could make him frighten and conquer the whole world for us.'

James overheard them and he told Young Monster.

'But I don't want to frighten and conquer the world,' cried Young Monster, 'I thought we could all be friends. And I want to be free.'

'Then,' said James, 'you must go now, quickly – back to your home in the Lake where they can't reach you.'

Young Monster sighed, a very sad sigh.

'I suppose you're right,' he said, 'I must go back to the Lake. And they shall never find me again.'

So, the Monster said goodbye to James and slipped away to the quiet calm depths of the Lake. James never forgot Young Monster. He would often walk down to the lakeside when it was dusk and he would wave when the Monster came up to the surface for a brief moment then disappeared again.

Some people say the Monster lives there still. But, if he does, he is very, very careful never to let anyone catch more than a glimpse of him nowadays.

The Jumping Game

Once upon a time there was a very lively flea, who loved to hop, skip and jump. He said,

'No one in the world can jump higher than I can.'

There was also a smart young grasshopper. He, too, loved to hop, skip and jump, and he said,

'No one in the world can jump higher than *I* can.'

And then there was a sly fat frog, who sat quite still and he said,

'You say no one in the world can jump higher than you two can? Well, let's have a jumping game and then we shall see!'

The flea, the grasshopper and the frog agreed. They asked the King and every-one else to come and watch their jumping game.

The King said, 'I shall give a prize to the best one. Now what shall it be?'

His Majesty thought hard and then he said, 'I know, the winner shall marry my daughter, the Princess. It's about time someone married her.'

The flea, the grasshopper and the frog agreed.

First came the flea. He bowed to the King and he bowed to everyone else. He was most polite – because, you see, he always tried to mix with the best company.

The flea took a hop, a skip and a jump and up, up into the clouds went he. He jumped so high up into the sky it was unbelievable!

'Where is he? Where is that flea?' asked the King.

No one knew. No one could see him.

'Here I am! I'm right up in the sky,' squeaked the flea.

But no one heard him.

So the King said, 'No jump, I declare! If the flea can't be seen how do we know if he jumped at all?'

That was very unfair to the poor little flea. He was very disappointed.

Next came the grasshopper. Grasshopper was proud of his strong legs, his smart green coat and his good singing voice. Everyone could see and hear *him!* He was certain he would win. But he was in too much of a hurry. He took a quick hop, skip and a jump. He slipped and he bumped right up against the King's nose.

'No jump, I declare,' roared the King. He was very angry.

Poor grasshopper was disappointed!

Then it was the fat frog's turn to jump. He wasn't in a hurry at all. He sat so still and so quiet that everyone thought he must have fallen asleep. But oh no, not he, that sly old frog was thinking. At last, very carefully, he took a hop, a skip and a jump. He had jumped just a very little jump, just far enough to land upon the Princess's lap as she sat beside the King on her golden stool.

Everyone wondered what the King would say!

'Well done!' said the King to the frog. He was delighted.

'Yours is the best jump of all, because you have jumped up to my daughter, the Princess, and I say she is the highest in the land. No one could jump higher than that. So now you can marry her.'

'Thank you very much, Your Majesty,' said the sly old frog. He was well pleased with himself.

The Princess was quite pleased too. No one else had asked to marry her. Besides, in a fairy story she knew, the frog who married a Princess turned into a handsome Prince. She hoped her fat frog would do the same . . . but he never did!

As for the grasshopper and the flea . . . Poor flea! He could see that it is not always the best who win at games and other things. So he hopped away with the King's army and fought many battles in far-off lands.

The grasshopper was sad, too, for a while. Then he said,

'I may not be so good at jumping as I thought, but at least I can still sing about it.'

And he did. He went away. He travelled all over the world and he sang, all the rest of his days. And the song he loves best of all is the one about the flea, the grasshopper and the sly old frog.

Stripey Tiger

Stripey was a toy tiger. He belonged to a boy called Simon. Simon and Stripey always went everywhere together.

One hot summer's day, Simon's father took them both to the zoo. After they had seen the bears, the monkeys and the penguins, Simon said to Stripey, 'Would you like to see some *real* tigers, Stripey?'

Stripey said he would. So Simon's father took them into a building where the lions and tigers were just about to be fed. Simon, his father and Stripey, sat on a wooden seat, high up on a stone platform to watch.

Presently Simon's father said, 'Would you like an ice-cream Simon?'

'Yes, please!' answered Simon, who was feeling very hot and thirsty. He jumped up and ran off with his father, forgetting all about Stripey.

Stripey was so interested in watching the real tigers as they prowled up and down, lashing their tails against the iron bars of the cage, that for once in his life, he had forgotten all about Simon! The sun beat down through the glass roof. It was hot and stuffy. Soon all the people went out into the fresh air and Stripey was left alone with the tigers.

Stripey slipped down off the seat, stood up very straight and called to the biggest tiger.

'Please sir, I'm only a toy tiger, but could you teach *me* to prowl and growl and roar, like you?'

The biggest tiger looked at Stripey. 'Of course little fellow. I'll soon teach you.'

He threw back his head. He roared. He prowled and he growled. Then Stripey threw back his head. He roared and he prowled and he growled.

'Perfect!' purred the biggest tiger. 'Now just once more,'

They were making such a noise that Mr Pilkington, the Zoo Keeper, came running in to see what all the fuss was about. He said to the biggest tiger, 'That'll do, you've just had your dinner. Now be quiet!'

Stripey was frightened. 'Oh dear! He thinks I'm a *real* tiger. Oh I do wish I hadn't pretended to be one.'

Stripey slipped past Mr Pilkington and ran outside as fast as he could, into the bushes.

'Here, come back!' shouted Mr Pilkington, as he chased after Stripey.

Mr Pilkington bumped into an old lady, who was trying to find the Tea Pavilion. 'I think perhaps I'd better take you indoors ma'am,' he said, taking the old lady by the arm. He hurried her off to the nearest building which, luckily for her, was the Tea Pavilion.

Soon the Superintendent came to see what all the fuss was about. Mr Pilkington told him, 'There's one of the tigers out here somewhere. I must get him back inside.'

Meanwhile, quite hidden under the bushes, Stripey shivered with fright. He was worried because Mr Pilkington had been so angry with him. There was a rustling noise in the bushes behind him and Stripey trembled more than ever. Very slowly, something was creeping towards him – until BUMP! It was right up against him.

'Oh Stripey,' said a voice, 'I'm glad I've found you. I couldn't think what had happened to you.'

It was Simon. He picked Stripey up and hugged him tightly.

Now, just at that moment, inside the Lion House, the Superintendent was counting the tigers in their cages.

'One, two, three, four. Mr Pilkington,' he called, 'how many tigers should there be in these cages?'

'F-f-four,' stammered Mr Pilkington, and sure enough there *were* four. 'Then there isn't one missing after all.'

'Quite right,' said the Superintendent kindly. 'Now Mr Pilkington, you've been working very hard lately, so I think you'd better take a holiday.'

And Mr Pilkington did. He went away to stay with his sister, who keeps rabbits and pet mice. It was a nice change for him from looking after tigers.

Grimitty-Gree

There was once a wee manikin called Grimitty-Gree. He had made himself a house of grass and dandelion leaves, in a corner of Farmer Brown's meadow. Then Farmer Brown sent his cows to graze in the meadow. Clomp! Clomp! went their feet and Chomp! Chomp! went their jaws as they ate the fresh grass. Soon Grimitty-Gree's house was all crushed to pieces.

He sat down and cried.

'Why are you crying?' called a lark from high up in the sky.

'My beautiful house is all broken down and I've got no home,' sobbed Grimitty-Gree.

'Build another! Make it stronger, then it's sure to last much longer,' trilled the lark.

'What shall I use?' asked Grimitty-Gree.

'Mud and sticks are the best to make a snug and sturdy nest,' sang the lark as off he flew.

So Grimitty-Gree searched for mud and twigs until he came to Farmer Brown's garden, where there was a huge pile of sticks and leaves.

'This will make a strong house which no one can break,' he said happily.

Just as it was beginning to get dark, Grimitty-Gree's house of sticks was finished. He was tired and thirsty so he went off down to the stream at the end of the meadow to fetch some water to make himself some tea.

Now, Farmer Brown had piled up those sticks and leaves ready for a bonfire. While Grimitty-Gree was gone, Farmer Brown, with his children Ann and John, came to light the bonfire. He carefully lit the fire while John and Ann stood well back and looked on.

First little yellow flames appeared, then small puffs of smoke. Then up and up rose the flames, and higher and higher curled the smoke. When the bonfire was all burnt away, Farmer Brown went back to the farm. Ann and John were going to follow but, at that moment, Grimitty-Gree returned.

'Help! Help!' he shouted. He ran to the remains of the bonfire and stamped on the smouldering embers.

'What's that down by the bonfire?' said John.

He pointed a stick to where Grimitty-Gree was standing. Grimitty-Gree clutched at the stick and John lifted him clear of the ashes.

'Let me see,' called Ann, running forward. 'Oh how did you come here,' she asked Grimitty-Gree.

'First the cows crushed down my house of grass and leaves. Then the fire burnt my house of sticks. Now I've no home at all,' cried Grimitty-Gree. Big tears rolled down his cheeks.

'Well,' said John, who was a kind boy, 'we must find a new home for you . . .'

'And I know the very place,' interrupted Ann, excitedly.

She picked Grimitty-Gree up and ran back home. She went indoors and upstairs to her bedroom. In the corner was a doll's house with real furniture. There were beds with real sheets on them. There was even real food in the tiny kitchen. It was just right for Grimitty-Gree.

'This can be your house now, if you would like to stay,' said Ann.

'Oh yes please,' replied Grimitty-Gree. He was so happy because, as he said, 'Now, at last, I really have a very fine house of my *own*.'

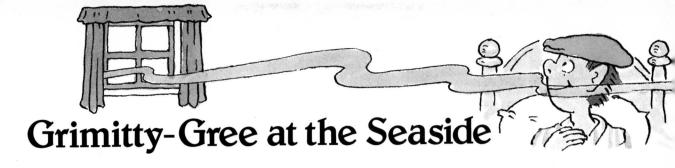

Grimitty-Gree at the Seaside

One bright and sunny morning, Grimitty-Gree woke up to the smell of chocolate cake cooking.

'Delicious!' he sighed happily. There was nothing he liked better than chocolate cake. Ann was sure to bring him a tiny piece as soon as it was cooked.

There was another happy surprise for him too.

'Come along, Grimitty-Gree,' called Ann skipping into the room with her red picnic bag swinging from her shoulder. 'We're going to the seaside for the day and we're taking a picnic with us.'

'If you're taking some chocolate cake,' said Grimitty-Gree, 'then I'll come too.'

'Yes we are,' laughed Ann, 'so come along.'

'But what *is* the seaside?' asked Grimitty-Gree, because he had never been to the sea before.

'Oh there are rocks and lovely sand and . . .'

'Hurry up Ann! We're going now,' called her brother John.

'You'll see when we get there,' Ann explained hurriedly, as Grimitty-Gree settled himself down inside Ann's bag.

All the way along in the car, he thought about the seaside and wondered what it would be like. After a while, Ann said excitedly, 'We're there!' And the children scrambled out of the car.

As they ran down to the beach, Grimitty-Gree could hear sounds which he had never heard before – the sad cries of the sea-gulls as they circled overhead, and the soft steady roar of the sea, as the waves ran over the sand. There was a strong tangy smell of fish and seaweed in the air, which was strange and new to him.

'Come and see,' Ann called to John. 'There's a little rock pool over here. We can play beside it and then hunt for sea-shells.'

Grimitty-Gree crept out of Ann's bag and, keeping well hidden among the rocks, he watched the tumbling waves making lacy patterns on the smooth gleaming sand.

'Take your shoes and socks off, then you can help us look for sea-shells in the pool,' Ann whispered to Grimitty-Gree.

Presently, 'Lunch-time!' called their father, and the children suddenly realized that the salt sea air had made them very hungry indeed. Grimitty-Gree was hungry too and he *was* looking forward to his piece of chocolate cake.

The sea-gulls swooped down when they saw the picnic food being taken out and Ann tossed a crust to one bird who caught it in the air as he flew.

'Oh how clever!' cried John.

But Grimitty-Gree didn't like the big white birds with their yellow beaks. They made him feel quite frightened. So he crept inside one of the children's sand buckets and hid there until the picnic was over. It wasn't until the last crumb had been eaten that Ann remembered Grimitty-Gree.

'Oh dear!' she whispered, when she found him at last, hiding at the bottom of the bucket. 'I am sorry Grimitty-Gree. I forgot all about your piece of chocolate cake.'

'Never mind,' replied Grimitty-Gree, bravely. 'Perhaps it wouldn't taste very nice with sand in it.'

But he really was very hungry.

'We'll build a sand-castle for you Grimitty-Gree,' said John. 'And you can have the rest of my ice-cream because sea-gulls don't like ice-cream.'

Ann and John built a magnificent sand-castle, with towers and turrets and high walls. Grimitty-Gree had a lovely time pretending he was the king of the castle and that he was defending it against an invisible enemy.

The afternoon went by all too quickly so that Ann and John were quite surprised when it was time to collect up their buckets, spades and shells and take them back to the car. It seemed all too soon for Grimitty-Gree too, who turned to take one last look at the sea, which was smooth and shining like a silver mirror in the late afternoon sunshine.

Just before she went to bed that night, Ann took some milk in a toy cup and a slice of chocolate cake to Grimitty-Gree in the doll's house.

'Wasn't it a happy day?' asked Ann.

'It was a lovely, lovely day,' sighed Grimitty-Gree happily. 'And this is a perfect end to a perfect day,' he said when she gave him the chocolate cake.

'In the morning,' said Ann, 'we'll get some glue and make some sea-shell flowers from the shells we collected today. Then on cold winter days we can remember all over again our happy day at the seaside.'

But Grimitty-Gree was fast asleep, dreaming about the seaside.

Brave Grimitty-Gree

Grimitty-Gree sat up suddenly in his little bed in the doll's house.

'There's somebody moving about downstairs. It must be burglars,' he said.

He sat quite still and listened. Yes, there *was* somebody downstairs. Grimitty-Gree could hear voices and someone moving about. Ann was fast asleep in her bed and, from the other bedrooms, he could hear the soft breathing of her parents and her brother John.

How could he warn them? He didn't want to wake the children and frighten them and besides, John always slept so soundly, it wouldn't be any good even trying to wake him! It was no good either trying to awaken their parents, because Ann and John were the only ones who knew about Grimitty-Gree.

'I'll have to go downstairs myself and see what I can do,' said brave Grimitty-Gree.

He jumped out of bed, ran across the dark landing and hurried downstairs, as quickly and as quietly as he could. When he was half-way downstairs, he peeped through the banisters and saw, in the sitting-room, two men with a torch, searching through the drawers of the desk.

'The money must be here,' one was saying to the other. 'He always gets the money for the wages from the bank on a Friday and he must have put it in here somewhere.'

As they searched, they threw all the papers out into a heap in the middle of the room, so that it looked as if there had been a gigantic paper snow-storm.

'How dare they!' thought Grimitty-Gree. 'Coming here and stealing the Browns' money and making such a muddle of everything.'

If only he could stop them.

'Never mind about the money,' snapped the younger of the two men, 'we'll take some of the other stuff instead.'

He had gone across to the sideboard and was filling a bag with everything he could lay his hands on.

'Leave that alone and come back here and help me, Bill,' growled the other. Bill dumped the bag down on the floor and, scuffing his feet through the papers, went back over to the desk to continue the search.

'Now's my chance,' thought Grimitty-Gree, feeling in his pocket for his tiny penknife. 'I'll cut a hole in his bag, so that if they do manage to get away, they won't get very far before all the things drop out.'

Instead of his penknife, he drew out of his pocket a silver whistle.

'Even better!' he exclaimed, for it was a special kind of whistle, which humans can't hear, but animals can. Jep and Rusty, the dogs who slept in the yard would come running when they heard the whistle. But how could he let them in? He could never pull back the great bolts on the outside doors all by himself.

'Of course! Why didn't I think of that before,' he said. 'The french windows. That's how they must have got in.'

The windows were right beside the desk. The burglars had pulled over the thick curtains so that no light should shine out through the windows, but the wind was moving the curtains slightly so that Grimitty-Gree knew the windows were still open.

His heart was beating very fast as, keeping close to the wall and well hidden in the shadows, he crept quietly across to the window. He pushed against the windows with all his might and blew on his silver whistle as hard as ever he could.

Immediately, *all* the animals on the farm woke up. The cock crowed, the hens squawked, the horses neighed, the cows mooed and the dogs barked loud enough to wake the whole village.

'Whatever's that!' cried Bill in alarm.

'Let's get out of here,' hissed the second burglar, picking up the bag and getting ready to run. But, just at that moment Jep and Rusty came bounding through the window so quickly that Grimitty-Gree was knocked over and lay hidden by the curtains, quite stunned for a while.

The dogs advanced towards the two

burglars, baring their teeth and growling dreadfully. The burglars backed away from the dogs and, as they did so, walked straight into Mr Brown and Constable Parslow, who had come to see what all the noise was about.

'Oh dear,' groaned Mr Brown later, after Constable Parslow had taken the two burglars away to the police station. He looked at the muddle of papers all over the floor.

'We'll have to clear that up in the morning.'

But, when Grimitty-Gree had recovered from his fall, he came out and stacked all the papers in a tidy pile before he went to bed. So that, at breakfast the next morning, Mr Brown said in astonishment, '*Someone* has tidied everything up. I wonder who it was?'

Ann and John smiled at one another and said nothing.

Grimitty-Gree's New Clothes

'Goodbye, Grimitty-Gree,' called Ann through one of the doll's house windows. 'We're just off for a picnic on the hills. I'll play with you when I come back.'

'Perhaps I shan't *want* to play,' said Grimitty-Gree sulkily, digging his heels into the patchwork rug in the doll's house sitting room.

'What's the matter?' asked Ann in surprise.

'Why can't I come too?' grumbled Grimitty-Gree. 'It won't be much fun for me here all by myself.'

'Oh poor Grimitty-Gree,' answered Ann quickly. 'It really would be better for you to stay here, because it is quite cold out on the hills and you know you've no warm clothes to wear. Unless you borrow some of the doll's clothes.'

Grimitty-Gree was feeling as grumpy as could be.

'No thank you,' he said, although he knew his green suit was as thin as paper, 'I don't want to wear any other clothes. Besides I shall be warm enough as I am.'

'Oh all right,' said Ann, holding open her shoulder bag. 'Hop in then quickly.'

Somehow everything seemed to go wrong that day, although Mrs Brown had chosen a lovely place for them to picnic, beside a sparkling stream which bubbled down the hillside into the valley below. While their parents rested, John and Ann played hide-and-seek with Grimitty-Gree among the golden bracken.

After a while, Ann said, 'I'm tired of this game. Let's play something else now.'

'We'll play "stepping-stones" across the stream,' suggested John.

John hopped across the stones, although they were rather wobbly. He scrambled up the muddy bank on the other side and turned to warn Ann.

'Careful,' he called, 'it's very slippery here.'

But, as he spoke, Ann lost her balance and toppled into the stream. Grimitty-Gree, who was just behind her, tried to catch hold of her dress to save her, and he too fell headlong into the water. Fortunately the stream was not very deep but the water was icy cold and both Ann and Grimitty-Gree were cold and shivery when they scrambled out of the water.

'We'd better go home right away,' said Mr Brown, when he saw Ann's wet clothes.

Next morning, 'Atishoo! Atishoo!' came from Ann's bed, and 'Atishoo! Atishoo!' came from the doll's house, just like an echo.

'You'd better stay in bed today, Ann dear,' said her father, as he carried Ann's breakfast up on a tray. 'Shall I bring you something to play with?'

'Yes please. May I have my sewing box?' asked Ann, for she had just had an idea.

All that morning, she cut and stitched away at some scraps of cherry-coloured woollen cloth, which her mother had given her. And all that afternoon, she knitted away with a ball of white fluffy wool and the smallest knitting needles she could find. By early afternoon her fingers were quite sore and her eyes were so tired that, when her mother came in later and said, 'What a fine little coat and muffler you've made,' Ann didn't hear her, because she was fast asleep.

Grimitty-Gree wasn't asleep, and when Ann's mother had gone downstairs, he came out to look at the new coat and muffler. They looked so warm and cosy, he just had to try them on. But, the red coat was so big that he was quite lost inside it and the white muffler was so long that it would have wrapped round his ankles and tripped him up.

'Oh dear, after she's worked so hard too,' murmured Grimitty-Gree. 'I wonder what we can do about it?'

Next morning Ann ran out on to the landing calling to her mother.

'Mummy, have you seen the little red coat and muffler I made yesterday? I can't find them anywhere.'

'No dear,' answered her mother, from downstairs, 'unless I picked them up with the washing.'

'Oh my goodness!' she said, as she took the things out of the washing machine, 'I'm afraid I did and they've shrunk up very small.'

'Never mind,' answered Ann, as she pegged out the red coat and white muffler on the clothes line. 'They look as if they are just the right size now.'

And they were. They fitted Grimitty-Gree exactly.

Grimitty-Gree's Christmas

It was Christmas Eve morning and Ann was up very early.

'Grimitty-Gree,' she called.

There was no answer. The front door of the doll's house was closed and the thick red curtains tightly drawn.

'That's odd! Perhaps he's still asleep,' thought Ann. 'Never mind, I can finish making his Christmas present and hide it away before he wakes up.'

Now Ann had gone out shopping with her mother, and Mrs Jellicoe, who helped with the cleaning, was busy in the hall when Grimitty-Gree got back. Grimitty-Gree was just going to creep up the stairs when Mrs Jellicoe suddenly saw him.

'Dear, dear,' she grumbled, for she was rather short-sighted, 'another decoration off the Christmas tree!'

She bent down and picked him up. Then she took a piece of string from her apron pocket and, carrying Grimitty-Gree over to the tree which stood just inside the dining-room, she tied him tightly on to one of the prickly branches.

But Grimitty-Gree *was* up. He had got up long before Ann was awake that morning. He had put on his warm red coat with the hood and his thick white muffler and gone to Stardale Woods to find some shiny holly berries and pine needles to make a necklace for Ann. He worked hard gathering the brightest berries. When he had strung them together, he popped them into the sack, which was slung over his shoulder and set off for home.

Grimitty-Gree did not like it at all. The pine needles pricked through his red coat into his back like daggers. But he had to keep as still and as quiet as possible because Ann and her brother John were the only people in the house who knew he could talk and move about. Mrs Jellicoe closed the dining-room door and went on with her work.

When Ann came home, she hurried upstairs. She called again to Grimitty-Gree and there was still no answer.

'I wonder where he can be,' she said. But she was so busy helping to get everything ready for Christmas morning that she forgot about Grimitty-Gree, until it was nearly bedtime.

She called him and she tried to peep through the drawn curtains into the doll's house, but there was no sign of him at all. She felt quite worried about him, so that when her father came to kiss her goodnight, he could see there was something wrong.

'Cheer up Ann,' he said, giving her a hug. 'Come downstairs for a minute and see how pretty the lights on the Christmas tree look now it's dark.'

Ann went downstairs slowly. Then, as she stood by the dining-room door, she caught sight of Grimitty-Gree in his red coat all tied up on a branch of the tree. The prickles were sticking in his back harder than ever and he felt very wretched indeed.

'Oh Grimitty-Gree!' she exclaimed, before she could stop herself. 'Daddy, please take him off the tree.'

Her father laughed. 'The little Father Christmas, do you mean? All right, I'll take him down for you now.'

When she got upstairs, Ann made a little mattress of cotton wool for Grimitty-Gree and rubbed his aching back for him.

'There,' she whispered, 'you'll be quite better in the morning, especially when you see my lovely Christmas present for you.'

Grimitty-Gree woke on Christmas morning feeling well again and he was delighted with Ann's present. She had made him a winter garden from an old dish her mother had given her. She had covered some bare twigs with glitter, which sparkled like real frost and fastened them into plasticine. She had put moss and fir cones round the edge of an old mirror, which looked like a frozen pond and had made mock snow with cotton wool and sprinkled that with glitter, too.

'Oh thank you, Ann,' exclaimed Grimitty-Gree delightedly, skipping round the mirror pond. 'Now look under your pillow and see if you like *my* present!'

Just then, Ann's father came in.

'What a lovely little garden you've made Ann,' he said. 'May we borrow it please for a table decoration today?'

'Yes, of course, Daddy,' replied Ann.

As the family all sat around the table for Christmas dinner, Ann's mother said,

'I do like your Christmas garden Ann and that little Father Christmas fellow looks quite real.'

Ann smiled across at her brother John, as she proudly stroked her new necklace. Grimitty-Gree, standing as still as a statue in his bright red coat and thick white muffler by the edge of the mirror pond, winked at them both.

April Fools

Once there were two silly old twins, Cuthbert and Colin. They looked exactly alike. They dressed exactly alike and they both did the same stupid things. They were both rather lazy too. They never bothered to think very much, so they were always getting into trouble.

You would hardly believe some of the daft things they did! For instance, one morning they both got up late and both were in a very bad temper.

'It's all your fault, you silly twin,' snarled Cuthbert, 'you overslept!'

'No it isn't and so did you,' snapped Colin.

'No I didn't!'

'Yes you did!'

'No I didn't!'

'Yes you did!'

And so they went on. The truth was they had a cuckoo alarm clock which they had both forgotten to wind up the night before.

'It's that clock's fault,' grumbled Cuthbert. 'It's stopped and it should have woken us up at seven o'clock'

'Then I'm going to teach it a lesson,' growled Colin, and he hit it hard with his fist. Then he kicked it. 'There! It won't do that again.'

Well, of course, it didn't do *anything* again, because Colin had broken it. So every morning they got up later and sometimes they snored their way right through the whole of one day and half-way through the next.

Until one lovely sunny morning in April, from the woods across the way, came:

'Cuckoo! Cuckoo!' seven times. And Cuthbert and Colin woke up with a start.

'What was that?'

They looked at the clock, which always said seven o'clock now – ever since Colin had broken it. Then they looked at each other.

'My goodness!' exclaimed Cuthbert, leaping out of bed and rushing to the window. 'It must be a flying alarm clock!'

'Don't be silly,' replied Colin scornfully, 'of course it isn't! It's a real bird. They only come for a short time in the year then they fly away again. But do you know what?'

'No what?' asked Cuthbert.

'We're going to catch it and keep it in our bedroom.'

'Of course!' agreed Cuthbert. 'It'll be much better to have a real bird to wake us up every morning than a useless clock that doesn't go.'

So they began to get dressed as fast as they could. As they were getting dressed, Cuthbert asked.

'How shall we catch it?'

'That's easy!' replied Colin. 'You just creep around the woods and find which bush it sits in, while I go down to the village with my wheelbarrow.'

'Oh all right,' said Cuthbert and he wondered what Colin was going to fetch from the village.

So off went Colin with his wheelbarrow down the lane to the village and off went Cuthbert to the woods, with a piece of white chalk. Round the woods he went in search of the cuckoo. Until from the old oak tree came the call 'Cuckoo! Cuckoo!'

'Oh so there you are,' murmured Cuthbert, 'now I've got you my little beauty.'

Very slowly and very carefully, so as not to make any noise, Cuthbert crept over to the oak tree and marked it with his chalk. But no sooner had he done this than, 'Cuckoo! Cuckoo!' off flew the bird to another tree.

This happened again and again until Cuthbert's piece of chalk was worn away to a little tiny stump. He grew so hot and tired from running from tree to tree, he thought he would go back home to have a short rest.

He had just sat down in the shade of the chestnut tree in the garden when Colin came puffing down the path with his wheelbarrow full of bricks.

'Cuckoo! Cuckoo!' sang out the bird yet again. And there it was, perched on a bush in the garden just nearby.

'That was clever of you to get him on that bush,' whispered Colin. 'Now quickly, we'll build a wall round him with these bricks so he can't get away.'

The cuckoo sat in the bush and put its head first on one side and then on the other, as it watched Colin and Cuthbert working away in the hot mid-day sun, making a wall as fast as they could around the bush.

'We've got him now!' panted Cuthbert, as pleased as Punch, as he put the last brick on top of the wall.

'Yes,' puffed Colin. 'Now let's sit down and have a rest.'

They threw themselves down on the grass, quite worn out with all their hard work. Then the cuckoo spread its wings and flew up above the wall, up and away into the clear blue sky.

'Cuckoo! Cuckoo!' he called as he flew, and it sounded as if he was laughing at them.

'Oh!' groaned Colin.

'Oh!' gasped Cuthbert, 'I didn't expect him to fly out at the top, did you?'

'No,' agreed Colin, looking very glum.

'And do you know what I think?' went on Cuthbert.

'What?'

'We're just a couple of April fools.'

Then both those two silly old twins began to cry, until Colin blew his nose, dried his tears and said,

'Do you know what Cuthbert? We could get our alarm clock mended. Then we could get up early and make something sensible with all those bricks.'

'Yes,' agreed Cuthbert, stretching himself out more comfortably on the grass. 'Let's just stay here until we think of something sensible.'

I wonder if they ever did, don't you? For all we know, they are lying there still – trying to think of something sensible.

Snip-snap-gobble-down-quickly

Of all the extraordinary creatures born upon the banks of the Umgakki River, Snip-snap-gobble-down-quickly was the most extraordinary of all. Even her own mother had said,

'I shall call her Snip-snap-gobble-down-quickly because she's *so* greedy.'

Everything she ate, she swallowed whole.

Now, one day, some scientists came to the Umgakki River. The Youngest Scientist had travelled all over the world looking for extraordinary animals. He had heard about the strange Snip-snap who lived by the Umgakki River. All the animals had heard about the Young Scientist and *they* moved off down the river as fast as they could. All, that is, except Snip-snap, who stayed just underneath the water by the bank watching them as they set up their camp.

The men unpacked food from a large black bag and began to prepare a a meal.

'Ummmmm', sniffed Snip-snap, 'that smells good enough to eat.'

Next to the black bag was a smaller bag. Snip-snap smiled a cunning smile as she glided closer to it. Then, with a swish of her tail, a flash of her teeth and a snip-snap-gibble-gobble, she had swallowed the bag in one gulp.

Now, Snip-snap had made a great mistake. She was wrong in thinking there was food in that bag. It was packed with all the medicines for the journey. So, first of all, Snip-snap felt very odd, then she felt very sleepy, because amongst the medicines was a box full of sleeping tablets.

Very soon Snip-snap was sound asleep. It was not long before the scientists noticed her.

'Look, there's a splendid creature! Bring the nets! We must take her home with us at once.'

The men hauled her out of the water and back to the aeroplane. But they could not get her inside, because she was so huge and *very* stiff from swallowing all that medicine.

'She'll have to be tied on to the undercarriage,' said the Youngest Scientist.

Now, the Youngest Scientist could only tie granny knots and, as the aeroplane soared away into the clouds, his knots got looser and looser. Until, slither-slither-splash, the rope slipped off and down fell Snip-snap into the sea.

Even this did not wake Snip-snap. She drifted along on the waves and was washed up upon the shore of a strange island. Of course, Snip-snap had no idea where she was. How could she? She was still asleep. She did not know that there was a storm raging all around her.

'Wheewish!' shrieked the wind through the trees.

'Splash, splish!' The rain pattered down upon Snip-snap's back.

'Crash, crish!' Branches were snapped off and blown down all over the island.

Now all this time Snip-snap had been dreaming of food, so that when a tree branch fell down upon her nose, sleepily, Snip-snap opened her mouth and took a large bite. Then she tried to swallow it, but, oh dear, what do you think? She could not. Her teeth were stuck fast. The branch, you, see, was from the effote tree which is a very soft and sticky tree and, when it gets wet, it's even softer and stickier – just like melted toffee.

Now the storm was so bad that the scientists' plane was forced to land on the very same island. So that when Snip-snap opened her eyes, there were the scientists, standing all around her.

115

Snip-snap would have loved to eat one of them but she could not even open her mouth. Tears came into her eyes.

'The poor beastie, she's crying,' said the Youngest Scientist, 'we must do something to get her teeth unstuck. Where's my medicine bag?'

All the men looked everywhere for it. But they couldn't find it. They could not think where it could have gone.

'Ah well,' said the Youngest Scientist at last, 'we must get her to an animal hospital as soon as possible.'

At the animal hospital back home, Snip-snap was put to sleep and the piece of wood was soon taken out of her teeth. But the next day, when the Youngest Scientist came to see how Snip-snap was, he said,

'Oh dearie me! The beastie's still not well. She looks to me as if maybe she has a terrible pain in her tum.'

So the Youngest Scientist asked for an X-ray picture to be taken of Snip-snap's stomach and sure enough:

'Why, there's my medicine bag!' cried the Youngest Scientist, when he saw the X-ray picture.

And that wasn't all. There were all kinds of other things which Snip-snap had swallowed – a gold watch, a fur coat, a snake-skin handbag, a pair of leather sandals *and* an umbrella. No wonder Snip-snap felt ill.

When she was quite better at last, Snip-snap was put in a large enclosure in Alltown Wild Animal Park. Lots of people come to see her now. But there is a big notice outside which says:

PLEASE DO NOT FEED THIS ANIMAL
especially with medicine bags.

And, there is another notice which says:

PLEASE STAND WELL BACK
if you are wearing a fur coat, gold watch, leather sandals, carrying a snake-skin handbag and an umbrella.

Visitors do stand well back, because they know that, true to her name, Snip-snap would snip-snap-gobble-them-down-quickly, if she could only get the chance.

Clever Old Foxy

High up in the hills, quite hidden by the trees, lived an old foxy fox in his den. It was a lovely place to live. That old foxy fox could look down and see the stream where the ducks came to swim. He hardly ever came down to try and eat them! He would wink his eye and say:

'I bother nobody and nobody bothers me
Because that's the way I like to be.'

Old Foxy was very happy with his way of life until one day along came a tickly, tetchy flea with his new little flea wife.

'Why my dear,' said Mr Flea to Mrs Flea, 'here's the very place for you and me to set up home and bring up a fine family.'

Together Mr Flea and Mrs Flea hopped upon old Foxy's back and settled down happily in the fox's warm golden fur.

At first old Foxy hardly noticed the fleas were there at all. He could still wink his eye and say:

'I bother nobody and nobody bothers me
Because that's the way I like to be.'

But after a while, there was more than just Mr Flea and Mrs Flea. There were hundreds of little fleas – all very naughty and very noisy. They hopped and they ran. From morning till night, they quarrelled and they fought. They played football and hide-and-seek. They held flea circuses and flea-markets. They

117

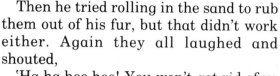

Then he tried rolling in the sand to rub them out of his fur, but that didn't work either. Again they all laughed and shouted,

'Ha,ha,hee,hee! You won't get rid of us so easily!'

So old Foxy lay down among the long cool grasses. He stayed quite still until a bright idea came to him. Then he jumped up and ran around under the trees. In his mouth he gathered up all the soft green moss he could find.

tickled and tormented that old Foxy from the top of his head to the tip of his tail.

Old Foxy tried to reason with them,

'Please go away,' he said, 'I bother nobody, so please don't bother me. That's the way I'd like to be.'

But those naughty fleas just laughed and said,

'Ha,ha,hee,hee! You won't get rid of us that easily!'

So old Foxy said to himself,

'I will have to think of some way of getting rid of those troublesome fleas.'

First he tried shaking himself very hard to make them all fall off, but they didn't. They all laughed and shouted,

'Ha,ha,hee,hee! You won't get rid of us so easily!'

The little fleas were much too busy being as naughty and as noisy as usual to notice what old Foxy was doing. Still carrying the soft green moss in his mouth, old Foxy went down through the trees until he came to the stream. The ducks swimming there were afraid old Foxy had come to eat them.

'Quack, quack, ducky dears, what shall we do? Has old Foxy come to make a meal of me, or of you?'

But old Foxy didn't even look at the ducks. He turned his back upon them.

The ducks watched old Foxy walking backwards into the water, carrying the moss in his mouth.

'Quack, quack, ducky dears, what is he up to?'

They decided it was safer for them not to stay. So the ducks flew away at once. Old Foxy waded deeper and deeper into the stream. When the water covered his tail, the fleas all hopped along old Foxy's back. Then when the water nearly covered his back, all those naughty, noisy fleas shouted.

'Ha,ha,hee,hee! You won't get rid of us so easily!' They hopped off old Foxy's back and up on to his nose.

But soon the water had reached old Foxy's nose. The fleas didn't like this one bit. They ran round and round trying to keep out of the water. Until one of them saw the piece of moss in old Foxy's mouth.

'Look! If we all jump on to that soft green moss, we'll be as safe and as snug as bugs in a rug. This old Foxy fox can't get rid of *us* that easily.'

All together the fleas hopped on to the moss. Just as the very last one leapt off his nose, old Foxy opened his mouth and let the moss, and all the fleas with it, float away down the stream.

Then he winked his eye and said:

'I bother nobody and nobody bothers me Because that's the way I like to be.'

Then he swam back to the water's edge. He climbed out and shook himself dry. Old Foxy went back to his den among the hills where he danced and sang all by himself in the sunlight.

The Field of Gold

Dozy Willie Donaldson was the laziest man in the whole world. His wife was always telling him so. Night and day she would be nagging him to dig or plant their one field which was full of nothing but weeds.

'Now there's Mick Marshall,' she said. 'He's a fine man to be sure. Up every morning at the crack of dawn, working his fingers to the bone. Now why can't you be more like him?'

Dozy Willie would scratch his head, wrinkle his freckled nose and say,

'I'll think about it, Mollie my love, my angel, I'll think about it.'

Willie would wander out to his field, lean on the gate and gaze at it for hours and hours. Then he would stroll up the hill to Mick Marshall's farm, lean on *his* gate and watch Mick working his fingers to the bone, for hours and hours. For, as Willie always said, there was nothing he enjoyed better than watching *someone else* working.

But one day, when his wife had been nagging him all the morning, Willie suddenly looked her straight in the eye and said,

'I'd tell you, wife, why I haven't dug that field, but I don't think you could keep a secret.'

'Not keep a secret!' screeched his wife. 'Why every secret in the village is safe with me.'

'I daresay,' smiled Willie, putting his feet up on her clean chair covers and settling down for a nap.

'Then tell me now,' she said, knocking his feet down off the chair with the end of her broom.

Willie could see he would get no peace until he had told her.

'Well,' he whispered, his eyes all big and blue and round, 'there's gold in that field of mine. So, now you know, don't tell a living soul.'

'As if I would!' said his wife, indignantly. 'And how do you know there's gold there?'

'Oh-h!' yawned Willie. 'Take my word for it, I've seen it, you can be sure of that. Now remember, it's a secret! So you're not to tell anyone at all.'

'Never!' she replied.

Then presently she went upstairs, put on her hat and coat and said to Willie,

'Willie, I have to go across to Mrs Marshall to borrow some flour to make a cake, but I won't be long.'

'Oh very well, my love,' murmured Willie. He put his feet back on the easy chair and was soon snoring his head off.

Willie's wife hurried across to Mick Marshall's farm as fast as her legs could carry her.

'Well, now Mollie dear,' smiled Mrs Marshall as she gave Willie's wife the flour 'has that lazy husband of yours started to dig his field yet?'

'Oh no,' replied Willie's wife, 'and I'll tell you the reason why, if you'll bend your head a little this way. Willie says it's a great secret so you must promise not to tell a soul.'

Mrs Marshall listened with great interest and, as soon as Willie's wife had left, Mrs Marshall hurried to the field where Mick was working, for she had something very important to tell him.

'Mick,' she said, 'just listen to what I've heard. Willie's wife told me herself that . . .'

121

Her voice sank very low as she whispered Willie's secret to her husband.

About a week later, Willie Donaldson's wife came into the kitchen to find Willie busy counting a great pile of money. He looked up at her with a big grin.

'Mollie, my love,' he said, 'I won't need to think about digging that field now. Look, we're rich! Although why Mick Marshall should want to buy *my* field beats me!'

'You fool, Willie Donaldson,' snapped his wife, 'he wants the gold in that field. That's what he's after.'

'Oh no,' laughed Willie, 'he won't even notice it's there! He'll dig it all up without even noticing.'

'What do you mean?' demanded his wife.

'Buttercups, Mollie my love. That field of golden buttercups was like a field of gold to me. I could watch the sunlight on that field for hours and hours. But I shall enjoy watching Mick Marshall working his fingers to the bone, for there's nothing I enjoy more than . . .'

'Oh no you won't!' snapped his wife. She snatched up the pile of money from the table and slipped out through the kitchen door with it.

'Where are you going with that Mollie my angel?' asked Willie.

'I'm going to Mick Marshall's,' called his wife over her shoulder as she hurried up the path.

'But you can't give it back!' cried Willie, struggling to catch her.

'Oh no. I'm not going to give it back,' she laughed, as she raced up the hillside, 'there's enough money here to buy *his* farm for *you*. And there's nothing I shall enjoy better than watching you working on it.'

'No! No! Come back!' called Willie, as he puffed after her. But his legs weren't used to moving so quickly and, as he saw her disappear into Mick Marshall's front porch, he said to himself with a sigh,

'Oh Willie, my lad, you'll be the hardest working man in the whole world from now on.'

THE END